THE WORLD WE LEFT BEHIND

Slavery divided us like we were two races, but really, we were always one—the human race

A Novel

ANDREA BLACKSTONE

*For Queen Jackson Haley, my great-grandmother
who was enslaved at a plantation in Alabama,
and each ancestral inspirer from a host of families
who paved the way for me to tell this story.*

PUBLISHER'S NOTE
This is a work of fiction. Names, characters, places, and incidents are either the product of the author's imagination or are used fictitiously, and any resemblance to actual persons, living or dead, business establishments, events, or locales is entirely coincidental.

ISBN: 978-0-9746847-4-1

First paperback printing, August 2025

Book Cover and Interior Design by: TWASolutions.com.

Acknowledgments

Without God, nothing I do would be possible. Thank you for keeping me strong and faith-filled.

To Darrin:

I cannot fathom what my life would be like if I had not met "the best guy ever." Thank you for caring about me and investing in my well-being. Without your help, this book would not exist. You were the first person to read any of it, and I haven't forgotten your sacrifices.

To my family:

I must acknowledge the ancestors who gave me permission to tell this story. I am especially grateful to my uncle, Alex Haley, who opened the door for me to become interested in history, identity, and genealogy. Special thanks to Michael Blackstone, Cousin Bill, and others who encouraged me to move forward with this project. Grandpa Simon, I admire you deeply, even though I was too young to remember you. Your parents' story helped shape this novel. I will remain forever grateful to my parents, Lois Ann Haley Butts and Alfred Blackstone. I strive to make you both proud. I'm sorry that neither of you will be physically present when this becomes a book.

To my friends:

Nneka and Yolanda, I am extremely grateful for the time you took to serve as beta readers. To my other friends who encouraged me over the years, thank you as well.

To my past, current, and future readers:

I greatly appreciate your support of my work. Thank you to those who nudged me now and then, asking when I'd return with a new book.

To my mentors:

Mr. Trotter, Dr. Z., Dena Wane, Mrs. Bramble, and Dr. Ruthe Sheffey—thank you.

To my editor and designer:

Jessica Tilles, I consider you both a businesswoman and a friend. Thank you for being the right person to bring this project to life.

To my photographer and son:

Thank you, Tyler Stallings. I appreciate your willingness to photograph cotton fields on a hot day. You have so much potential—never give up.

To future supporters:

Thank you in advance for helping to get this story into the hands of more people.

"Freedom is telling the truth from all sides,
even if most people would rather avoid the topic."

—Andrea Blackstone

1

Children of the Plantation

The Rutherford Rocks Plantation, circa 1850s

Rutherford Rocks, an eight-hundred-acre plantation in Alabama, stood among towering, longleaf pines and fertile soil where cotton and tobacco once thrived. White settlers seized the land from Indigenous peoples and carved it into a profitable estate. Enslaved workers—who comprised forty-five percent of Alabama's population by 1861—used their skilled labor to build the plantation, laying the foundation for its enduring presence. Their forced labor fueled the brutal efficiency of the cotton industry, a lucrative enterprise that demanded a vast workforce to maintain Alabama's status as one of the nation's leading cotton producers.

The transatlantic slave trade shattered African cultures, reducing people to mere commodities. Slave traders chained and packed captive Africans onto ships that crossed the ocean, destined to toil in fields under ruthless overseers. At

Rutherford Rocks, work began before sunrise for more than one hundred enslaved laborers under the ownership of John A. and Catherine M. Brower.

The vast continent of Africa—known as the Mother of all civilizations—evoked images of ancient power, vibrant cultures, and rich landscapes filled with thriving kingdoms and flourishing communities. Before the transatlantic slave trade bound millions in chains, African kings, queens, and strong tribal bonds shaped a proud and diverse heritage. Conflict emerged when rival tribes captured prisoners of war and traded them for rare imports. Coastal traders sold debtors and criminals, forcing them to endure a perilous ocean journey. Even powerful African kings, unaware of the cruelty that awaited their people, sometimes exchanged them for goods.

The captives could never have imagined the torment that awaited them. In Africa, slavery existed, but not on this level. On ships, leg irons restrained them, and the cat-o'-nine-tails—a whip with knotted lashes—delivered brutal punishment. To prevent escape, enslavers branded people with hot irons, marking them with their "owner's" initials. They used iron muzzles, punishment collars, and masks to inflict even more pain. People traded the spirit of God once alive in their hearts for the worship of wealth, allowing greed to overshadow the Most High.

The strongest among the enslaved endured an eighty-day voyage to a grim new homeland. At least two million perished from dysentery, disease, starvation, or suicide—some leaping into the sea to escape their fate. Among the cargo were African food crops, including millet, yams, cowpeas, and plantains, which enslaved Africans had brought with them during their forced transportation. As they faced the horrors of forced displacement, some African women tucked kernels of rice into their hair—an act of quiet resistance and preservation, ensuring their culture could survive the journey into bondage.

A new generation of enslaved people grew up in America, where slave owners' wealth multiplied while erasing African identities. Rosalind and Bradley Wesbury were born of this poisoned legacy—a mixture of Southern oppression and African blood. In the pre-Civil War South, two families bore the names Brower and Wesbury: the White owners and the Black descendants, the "children of the plantation." John Brower II's blood—an unwelcome truth—ran through their veins, tangled in the slave birth index.

Rosalind often saw the resemblance when she washed her face at dawn, her features mirroring those of the man who denied her existence. She hated looking more like her father than her mother, Hazel, whose deep brown skin was as smooth as chocolate pudding. Hazel's body bore the pain of years spent wielding hoes and bending over fields. Her daughter's mere existence was a reminder of the master's cruelty and his refusal to acknowledge his biracial offspring.

John Brower inherited only a few acres of land by the Alabama River, while his wife, Catherine, brought substantial wealth to their marriage. Yet, it was John who pursued fortune, expanding his wealth on the backs of the enslaved who toiled over three hundred acres. He was the wealthiest man in Alabama before the Civil War—a man with sunken eyes, a sharp tongue, and an icy heart. The cowhide whip on the table beside his bed was a constant threat. If an overseer hesitated, Brower would crack the whip himself until blood streamed down the backs of his "property."

Hazel's mother had been among those shackled and taken from Africa, arriving at Rutherford Rocks only to be torn from her infant daughter. She died between rows of cotton at a nearby farm when Hazel was just two years old. Hazel had only a vague memory of her father—a shadow in her mind, lost through no fault of his own.

∞

By sixteen, Hazel longed for a connection of her own, a chance to break the pattern of loneliness. She had blossomed into a vibrant young woman with curves, catching the attention of Henry, a healthy seventeen-year-old. They exchanged tender glances whenever they passed each other around the plantation. Henry had admired Hazel long before she reached womanhood but held back, fearing for her safety. Still, he couldn't stay away and finally made his intentions known.

Henry's skin, smooth and dark as onyx, stretched over a lean, muscular frame as though sculpted by divine hands. Henry's confident and kind qualities drew Hazel to him. One Sunday, on a rare day of rest granted to the enslaved, Henry recited a poem he'd crafted from memory.

"You need a break from doin' a man's work," Henry told her, his voice like honey, melting her heart.

Hazel imagined dancing with Henry in the parlor of the Great House, her dress swishing like the fine ladies she had seen at the master's balls. Unfortunately, the reality of their lives cut that daydream short.

Ever watchful of his property, John Brower spotted the two under a large oak tree where they shared their secret moments. When he saw Henry leaning in to kiss Hazel, jealousy flared in his chest.

Hazel's heart raced as she looked into Henry's eyes, searching for the love she desperately wanted to believe in.

"One day soon we gon' be together," Henry promised her.

"You love me?" Hazel's voice trembled with a mix of fear and hope.

"Dats the only way I gon' be wit' you."

Henry's gaze softened as the morning light touched Hazel's youthful face. For a fleeting moment, he felt a sense of peace—a rare reprieve from the weight of enslavement. He leaned in, his breath sweet, as he whispered, "Since the day I saw you, there's been no one more important ta me. You my best friend. No matter what happens here, promise me we always gon' love each other."

Hazel's eyes filled with tears. "You my best friend, too. I love you back an' always will."

Henry twirled Hazel around, her laughter ringing out as he held her close.

"Henry loves me!" She giggled as they fell into a patch of soft grass beneath an oak tree.

He pressed his body gently against hers, his lips brushing hers as a calm breeze swept by. For a moment, it felt like they were free.

"If I's asked you to jump da broomstick and have a fine family, would you let me love you?"

"What you think I should say, Henry?"

"Yessum, 'cause I's a good young man." He flashed a playful grin.

"Den dat's what my answer is." Hazel smiled brightly.

With his strong hand, Henry held hers as he envisioned a future where he could protect and provide for her. "Someday we get married, and we can move ta our own shack. I will work ta gives you a better life you be proud of."

"Just tells me when it gon' come true, and I jump da broom wit' my Henry!" She clasped her hands with joy.

However, their moment of bliss shattered when John Brower had been spying on them. His face twisted in rage, as he stomped forward, bellowing, "Get ya hands off my gal!"

The joy vanished from Hazel's face as the harsh reality of their lives came crashing back.

2

Broken Bonds

$\diamond\!\!>\!\!>\!\!>\!\!<\!\!<\!\!<\!\diamond$

Henry turned when he heard Massa Brower's voice—sharp, spitting, and full of irritation.

"Maybe ya didn't hear me when I said, 'Get ya hands off my gal!'" Brower's eyes narrowed into slits of anger.

Henry stood firm, the towering figure that Hazel had always seen as her protector. He refused to bow or show any fear. "Or maybe I's did hear ya, Massa. Dis' my girl, my love. Das all."

Massa Brower's face twisted with disdain, a sneer curling of his lip as he shoved Henry back, putting distance between him and Hazel. "What are you two doin' out here?" His eyes flickered between the pair.

Henry wanted to avoid a confrontation, so he stayed silent.

"I asked you a question," Brower pressed, stepping closer.

Henry met his glare. "And I didn't give ya no answer."

Brower's expression darkened. "Don't use dat tone with me, you sassy nigger!"

"Don't scare da lady," Henry shot back, rising to his full height.

Trembling, Hazel clutched her hands and hung her head. "Henry. Don't say nuttin'. Hush now."

But Henry couldn't keep his mouth shut. "Cracker," he muttered.

The word ignited a spark of fury in Massa Brower, cracking his fist against Henry's mouth with a sickening thud. Hazel flinched as the blow landed, her lip quivering as she turned away, unable to watch. When she heard the unmistakable sound of a whip being uncoiled, she let out a scream that pierced the air, raw and filled with agony.

Tears streamed down her cheeks faster than she could wipe them away. The sharp crack of the whip sliced through the humid air, and Hazel's heart ached with every lash. Massa Brower didn't hold back; he wanted to strip Henry of his dignity, to break him down with the sting of leather against flesh. Now on his knees, blood trickled down Henry's back, staining his shirt as he clenched his teeth, swallowing the pain like he'd done countless times before.

"You worth more alive than dead to me." Brower dropped the whip from his sweaty hands. "I can't give ya too many licks."

Hazel gasped, finally looking up. Her hands shook as she reached out for Henry, her warrior, her love, but there was no safe space for him on this plantation.

"Get back, gal. Let him be," Brower ordered.

Hazel, with a heavy heart, stepped away, knowing better than to disobey. The price of Henry's brave words was a bloodied back, and she wept until her stomach ached. The sight of his suffering made something inside her break, shattering the small sliver of safety she'd dared to feel.

"Don't cry for him! This nigger did it to himself, wit' his disrespectful mouth. He know da rules. Look what he made me do." He wiped the sweat from his ruddy face, his gaze filled with sick satisfaction.

Hazel glimpsed the devil inside Brower, lurking behind his corpulent body. Her mind went blank, caught in a trance. She wanted nothing more than to comfort Henry, to soothe his wounds with a cool rag, but she knew better. Massa was all about control, and he'd do whatever it took to maintain his grip on the enslaved.

Massa Brower summoned an overseer to send Henry back to the burning fields to pick cotton, sending a message: rebellion required punishment, and obedience enforced it. The cycle of brutality continued unbroken.

Henry and Hazel were nothing more than property to Brower, valuable only as currency. Rutherford Rocks stripped the enslaved of their humanity, reduced to heartbeats that served the profit margins of the plantation.

∞

Brower gripped Hazel's hand, squeezing her fingers with possessive force as he dragged her from the cook's quarters, pulling her down the hall of his pillared house. He pushed her into a room and shut the door, his intentions clear.

"You thought dis was over?" Brower taunted, moving closer to her. "Talk to me, gal."

"'Bout what?" Hazel backed up, cornering herself against the wall.

Brower moved in closer, his hot face warming her face as he gripped her arm, squeezing it, inflicting pain.

"Stop what yer' doin'. I didn't do nothin'." As much as Hazel wanted to fight him off she feared the repercussions of doing so.

"You's my property." Brower's voice dripped with venom. "Ya weren't where ya was s'posed to be."

"But it's Sunday, Massa Brower. It's a rest day for da slaves." Although desperation edged her voice, Hazel tried to remain calm, fearing he would inflict more harm.

"You ain't wife material. You can't legally marry Henry. If you don't give me what I want, I'll take it."

The room filled with a suffocating silence as Hazel realized the futility of her protests. Brower didn't believe enslaved people had a right to love unless he commanded it. He wanted her to submit, to accept the twisted role he had forced upon her.

Massa Brower's grip tightened as he forced Hazel to disrobe. Her hands instinctively covered her body, wanting to shield herself, but he pried them away. Hazel thought about the other slaves, knowing she wasn't the first or wouldn't be the last to endure this. Her body wasn't her own—not one inch of it. She belonged to Massa Brower. His property. To do with as he pleased.

The taste of Brower's kiss—salty and rough—repulsed her, a mockery of the tender love she shared with Henry. Hazel's heart cried out for him, but he wasn't there to protect her. At that moment, she felt the storm building inside her—a storm that threatened to tear apart the fragile threads of her spirit.

"You don't get to choose who you want to be with," Brower hissed. "Do what I say, or I'll have you shot."

Hazel swallowed hard, knowing he meant every word. In the eyes of the law, she was nothing more than his property.

Brower violated her, leaving her hollowed out and broken.

"That's a good gal." Brower chuckled. "You're all mine now."

"*No! No!*" Hazel's screams echoed in the small room, but her cries fell on deaf ears.

Brower dismissively waved at her. "There's no need to be dramatic." He took everything from her, leaving her trembling with a shattered spirit. He enforced control of Hazel while taking no less than everything that she had to give.

Hazel shook as Massa Brower's sweat clung to her skin, making her feel clammy, his stench erasing all traces of Henry's scent. A storm was brewing in her life like a hurricane approaching land. As the man who owned her abused her body, Hazel's only way of surviving the emotional trauma of the repulsive assault was imagining that she could see Henry's smile. However, the love of her life was nowhere around, and Henry was incapable of protecting her.

The mistress of the plantation would pay with tears for the sins of her husband. Catherine Brower was the true economic engine behind the financial success of Rutherford Rocks, even if no one realized she was the most powerful, brutal slaveholder who could deliver far worse deeds than her husband. Together, the damage they did was significant and devastating.

3

A Heart Divided

❦❯❯❯❮❮❮❦

Slavery demanded cruelty and submission, affording no mercy from planters who owned Negro flesh. Henry had endured a week's starvation while Massa Brower sought to subdue his spirit by weakening his body and mind. Massa Brower harbored the fear that the Negroes would one day seize arms and foment rebellion at the plantation. Henry possessed the demeanor of one who might incite an uprising. Thus, his tale at Rutherford Rocks would not be his to tell. He received only enough sustenance as would maintain his consciousness.

"Apologize for what you did, boy," Massa Brower told Henry, trying to make him docile.

His stomach churned; his body was weak. "Not taday, not ever. I fights for the person I's need to fight for."

"Don't be stupid. I said, 'apologize.'"

"No, suh."

"Then ya leave me no choice ta give ya what you got comin'," Brower said with the flick of a hand.

Henry suffered public flogging before a considerable assembly, Hazel among them. The sinister Massa Brower commanded her presence at the fore that she might witness Henry's disgrace and downfall. Brower deemed Henry's rebellious nature beyond tolerance, requiring swift correction lest such defiance spread among the hands at Rutherford Rocks. An overseer had previously broken Henry's teeth for his insolence.

"Since Henry so desperate for attention, les' all watch how he handle dis' beatin' he gon' get." Massa Brower swung the whip toward Henry's dark flesh. With each lash, Henry drew breath deep within his breast. "Do it hurt bad enough yet?" John Brower taunted him, with his whip in hand.

"I'm not yoz to kill. I belong ta God!" Henry screamed.

Hazel jumped at each blow. "Oh, Laaaaawd! May God save mys Henry!"

Hazel's heart cried that Henry's affection for her resulted in such torment. She wept and beseeched the Lord that Massa Brower recall Henry's worth as property, that he might spare him mortal harm. Henry stood ready to perish for his beloved.

Massa Brower grew weary, his inability to break Henry's spirit leaving him enfeebled. The Negro's insufficient terror frustrated him deeply. Henry's exceptional labor made his defiance all the more vexing.

"Boy, yous just too much trouble!" He dropped the whip.

"I's gon' be myself."

Hazel wept as Massa Brower commanded Henry to cleanse and oil his flesh in preparation for sale.

Henry departed the plantation in shackles, head bowed and spirit subdued, nevermore to glimpse his beloved Hazel. At market, Massa Brower positioned his property upon the auction block.

ൟ

The sun was unrelenting, beating down on the crowd gathered at the raised wooden platform where owners displayed their human wares. Dust swirled around the feet of the onlookers, a thick cloud of it kicked up by the impatient shuffling of boots. Henry stood in the middle of it all, shackled at the wrists and ankles, the iron biting into his raw skin. He could still taste the salt of his own sweat, mingled with the bitterness of blood from the split on his lip. His shoulders sagged as if the weight of every moment he'd spent on that plantation had finally settled into his bones.

He didn't dare look up. Meeting the eyes of those who came to bid on him would be to acknowledge the full measure of his fate. Instead, his gaze fell on the dirt below, where dried stalks of grass poked through cracks in the earth—just as desperate for freedom as he was. He could still see Hazel's face in his mind, the way her eyes had brimmed with tears when they had dragged him away. He never got to say goodbye. He never got to tell her that he'd loved her more than life itself.

Behind him, a sharp voice barked, "Step up, boy!"

Henry flinched, the movement making his chains rattle like a death knell. A rough hand shoved him forward onto the auction block. He stumbled, catching himself just before he fell. The crowd's murmurs grew louder, a mixture of curiosity and appraisal. It wasn't the first time they had seen a man broken.

The auctioneer, a tall man with a face weathered like old leather, raised his hand to silence the murmuring crowd. "Here we have a strong one." He gripped Henry's arm as if to prove his point. He spun Henry around, displaying him like a prized beast at a county fair. "Worked hard in the fields. Strong back, good for the heavy lifting. How much for this nigger, gentlemen?"

The crowd leaned in, eyes narrowing as they sized him up as one might inspect horseflesh. "Open your mouth," a potential bidder told him.

Henry kept his head bowed, refusing to meet their gaze. He felt their eyes roam over his body, appraising his worth in the same way they might appraise the muscle of a horse or the heft of a sack of grain.

"Fifty dollars!" shouted a voice from the back. The bid came without hesitation, like someone buying a loaf of bread.

Henry's fists clenched at his sides, knuckles whitening as he fought back the swell of rage and helplessness. He wanted to scream, to tear off the chains, and run back to Hazel—to reclaim a life others had stolen from them before it even began. But he stood there, shackled and subdued, as the auctioneer continued his song.

"Fifty! Do I hear sixty?" The auctioneer's sharp voice rang out, cutting through the murmurs like a blade.

A pause.

Then, "Sixty!" another bidder barked, this one closer.

Henry could feel their eyes boring into him, a sensation colder than the steel around his wrists.

He closed his eyes briefly, letting himself slip away from the present, if only for a second. He pictured Hazel's smile— soft, like the whisper of a spring breeze, the only thing that had ever felt like home.

The bidding climbed higher, each call hammering another nail into the coffin of his old life. He could hear the excitement building in the auctioneer's voice, sensing a good sale.

"One hundred! Do I hear one hundred and twenty?"

Henry finally looked up then, not at the faces of the bidders but at the open sky above, vast and blue, mocking his captivity. He took a deep breath, the kind of breath that made his chest swell with a fleeting sense of freedom, and then he exhaled, feeling the shackles tighten with the movement. He knew he might never see that sky again without chains weighing him down.

"One hundred and fifty!" The final bid came from a voice thick with satisfaction.

The auctioneer's gavel came down like an axe with a decisive thud. "Sold!"

It was done. Just like that. Henry was no longer a man; he was a transaction, a number scribbled in a ledger.

He stepped down from the block, his head still held low, as if he could hide from the world that had branded him as property. But in his heart, the image of Hazel lingered, a small flicker of hope in the darkness swallowing him whole.

"Move along!" a voice barked at him.

He shuffled forward, the chains rattling like the toll of a bell. The crowd dispersed, already turning their attention to the next poor soul dragged onto the platform. As his new owner led him away, Henry cast one last look back over his shoulder, a silent farewell to a life that was now lost to him forever.

"Now, you belong to me. Don't give me no trouble, boy," his new owner said.

∽∾

Hazel's countenance bore a piteous expression upon learning of Henry's fate.

"Trouble yaself over big things. Dis' not one of 'em," Massa Brower calmly told her.

Hazel's contemplation ceased at the appearance of Brower's wife, Catherine, whose visage darkened at the sight of her husband addressing a Negro with civility.

"Why would you talk kindly to a servant?" Catherine then looked at Hazel. "I used to be very fond of you. I've owned you a long time before you came here. You should know how to stay out of my eyesight. I was napping. You woke me up." Catherine smacked Hazel's face.

Hazel caressed her stinging cheek, trying to hold back the tears. "I's sorry, Missus!"

"You should be for being a lazy and dumb savage. Everything should've been cleaned hours ago. My room hasn't been swept and my chamber pot hasn't been dumped. Let me know when lunch is ready. You can clean up my room when I eat lunch. I know you have a habit of being slow, but try shocking me for once and get things done quickly."

Catherine had accompanied her father to slave markets since childhood. At five years of age, she selected her first Negro as casually as a frock from a milliner's window. "I want that one!" Catherine had said, sounding like she was picking out a pet.

With effortless grace, she withdrew, following the chastisement of her first companion, who had attended her since infancy. The day's labors of bidding upon Negroes for her husband's holdings had quite exhausted her.

She had conveyed three Negroes to Rutherford Rocks as part of her marriage portion, Hazel among them. The estate was her birthright. Her father, Charles Marshall, had prospered in the flesh trade. Catherine's three servants had attended her since her youth, bearing her caprices with dutiful forbearance. Through the law of coverture, a wife's property becomes her husband's upon marriage. However, the Mississippi Married Women's Property Law of 1839 permitted White ladies of marriage to retain ownership of Negroes.

Want and uncertainty had never touched Catherine's existence. Every door stood open to a genteel Southern lady of Christian virtue. Daily, her figure was adorned in fitted gowns of the finest cloth, while Hazel's crude garment of burlap scarcely surpassed a collection of rags.

Their families arranged the union between Catherine and Brower when she was fifteen years of age. Jane and Charles Marshall possessed tremendous wealth through their extensive holdings in Negro flesh and had groomed their daughters to embody the ideal of Southern womanhood. Their parents cultivated Catherine and Sarah Ann's charm, wit, purity, innocence, and social graces from their earliest steps. Jane's upbringing taught her to embrace the accepted beliefs of her time about the Negro race, and she wielded punishment with expertise. In her estimation, they possessed neither industry nor wit. Catherine inherited her mother's conviction that Negroes were soulless chattel, valuable only for the accrual of familial prosperity.

Catherine rolled her eyes at Hazel. She kissed her husband on the lips, flaunting their so-called relationship. As she walked away, Catherine smiled, bragging to her husband about the new slaves she'd purchased.

"They're going to make us a lot of money."

∞

Karma finds those who tempt it, no matter where or when. Catherine had long courted such retribution. Her comeuppance manifested when Hazel felt the quickening of new life within her belly. Nine months later, as a full moon illuminated the plantation, Rosalind drew her first breath. As Hazel's labor ceased, tears coursed down her cheeks, thoughts of Henry mingling with the bitter recognition that this child of Massa Brower's seed should have been their own.

The infant's fair complexion and features spoke plain testimony of her husband's transgression to Catherine's horrified gaze. The child's presence threatened grave complications at Rutherford Rocks, her appearance ill-suited to labor beside her mother in the fields.

"My God!" Catherine screamed, moving closer.

Malevolent thoughts consumed Catherine as she beheld Rosalind's pale flesh, irrefutable evidence that her husband had known their property in the biblical sense before she had borne him a child.

"Let me hold that baby," Catherine demanded, plotting the child's demise although she'd just been born.

A wild glimmer in her eye made Hazel refuse. She kissed her daughter and held the baby tighter. "No, Missus."

"You need my guidance. I don't need yours. I'm the lady of the house who has the right to name this infant."

A stout, older enslaved midwife appeared, standing in front of Catherine. Three more women, who felt the child was in danger, surrounded their mistress. Catherine stormed out of the slave quarters, rage-filled and foiled. Her wispy blonde hair framed her delicate face as a veil of tears coated her eyes. She found Massa and pounded him in the chest.

"I know what you did! I want both gone!" Catherine screamed at her husband.

"Both who?"

She was wide-eyed. "This bastard thing and your bed-wench, Hazel! How could you make me suffer by doing this?"

"Control yaself." John grabbed Catherine by the shoulders.

"You're trying to break me. I thought we were a team."

Tears blurred her vision as she collapsed on the floor. Catherine couldn't comprehend why her husband sought comfort with Hazel—a Negro woman adorned in coarse cotton and a headwrap concealing short, coarse-plaited hair. Catherine's coiffure rarely showed disarray. She remained blind to a simple truth: her rigid propriety denied John the spontaneity he craved. His time with Hazel recalled all the freedoms his wife had denied him, though Hazel's consent mattered not to him. Catherine deferred discussion of such matters, her breeding demanding a proper Southern lady's submission to her husband.

Standing ramrod straight, Catherine peered at John. "It's them or me."

"Don't make me choose, ya lose. My slaves are worth more than one wife."

"Our slaves," Catherine corrected, facing her husband.

John sucked his teeth. He didn't feel that women should have the right to own anything.

"You chose me. You married me. I was your very best choice and we both know it." Catherine sniffed, flashing her diamond ring.

After a decade of marriage, Catherine remained naïve to her husband's nature. He had sired other Negro children in his youth, all sold away with little ceremony. Their disposable status stemmed from their failure to reflect his likeness. Custom dictated the sale of both mother and child in such circumstances, sparing the master's wife's continued offense.

John glared at Catherine, reminding her that her gender made her his subordinate.

"Not another word. I's in charge of da slaves."

"How can that be? You didn't own any of them when we married."

John's manhood didn't crumble. He asserted his authority over his wife, warning her with the wag of a finger. "I's in charge of you."

Catherine took offense that her husband felt superior because she wore a dress, and he hadn't paid his own way to achieve a path to wealth. Nevertheless, Catherine tried to keep the peace. She slowly placed her hand on his arm and smiled. "I don't want to argue. Let this go."

"I'm always right, so don't eva talk ta me like that again. A wife should neva talk back to her man!"

He longed to inform Catherine that Hazel's domestic abilities far exceeded her own, though he spared her feelings on this account. Though Catherine remained ignorant of the fact, a Negro woman had captured her husband's affections.

4

The Queen of Nothing

❦>>><<<❦

A year had passed since Rosalind's birth. Catherine thought her husband would remain her one true love until he violated their marital sanctity. Catherine and John had once shared many late-night conversations when the plantation lay still and quiet, but their intimacy faded with time.

Most mornings, John told Hazel, "Meet me tonight as soon as da moon comes."

Catherine lit a candle, wondering where John had spent his hours. He spoke to her less than ever, absent more than present. Catherine found herself alone, and her efforts to maintain their bond felt futile. Her spirit withered as Hazel yielded to John's every command.

Catherine sat next to her husband on the bed. "I'm trying to make you happier."

"I gotta go." John bent down to slip on his leather shoes.

Catherine felt her husband was obligated to stay at home. With her frustration building, her cheeks flushed. "This isn't how you're supposed to act in a marriage. We haven't had a chance to talk, and you're gone at night too much. No one loves you more than I do! Why are you leaving me alone?"

"So, now our marital problems are my fault?"

"I never said that. I'll come, too."

Standing, he stretched. "Ya' can't."

"Why?"

"Ya' been doin' a good job not questioning a man. Now ya' doin' it again. Don't worry ya' pretty little head about where I's go, 'cause you know I'm comin' back. See ya' later. Get some sleep." John patted his wife on her soft cheek.

Upon hearing the front door open and close, Catherine rose from the bed and moved toward the window. Drawing back the curtain, she watched her husband follow a moonlit path to the slave quarters. He had wielded such control over Hazel that her spirit was broken. She spoke no more of Henry, mourning only John's absence.

John sought Rosalind and Hazel in the night hours, for Hazel fulfilled his desires more than his wife. He gazed at the stars through open windows, the pair in his embrace. Everything had changed since Rosalind's birth. Massa Brower's thoughts dwelled constantly upon them. He would lay beside them, kissing both mother's and daughter's brows until sleep claimed them.

Catherine sat alone in her fine mahogany bed, knowing she had disappointed her family. Though she wished for legal recourse, her husband's actions were sanctioned by law.

Try as she might, Catherine remained barren. Her family had arranged her young marriage to ensure heirs, to preserve their bloodline and traditions of racial separation. She believed a child might restore John's respect, though he had already sired one with enslaved women. John took what he desired while his true Southern belle wife suffered. Their wealth grew from the toil of slaves and bountiful crops.

Rutherford Rocks yielded sugarcane and corn alongside cotton and tobacco. Catherine's life of privilege turned bitter from her barren womb, though she had not yet seen thirty years. Despite her devotion as a Christian woman who faithfully sought the Lord in prayer, as her mother taught, God's blessing of children eluded her.

Each glimpse of Rosalind's smile brought fresh degradation. She awaited the child's maturity with dark purpose, imagining the day she might summon the girl with her bell, forcing her to serve as any other slave. Such were the only comforting notions she had.

Rather than treating her as chattel, Massa Brower made Rosalind his favorite. A comely child who bore her father's features, her presence reminded Catherine daily that the mulatto held a higher status than she. At Christmastide, Massa Brower moved his mistress and child from the quarters to the Great House, weary of his nightly journeys. He installed

Hazel as a house servant, granting her one of two privileged chambers near the longtime cook's quarters.

"We movin' in de great, big house!" Hazel exclaimed with joy.

In her youth, Hazel had slept at Catherine's bedside. Now she found rest away from the watchful overseer who demanded absolute obedience. Her crowded cabin lay just beyond view. Peace had eluded her until Massa Brower began rewarding her submission to his will.

"You are ruining the Brower's moral and social reputation," Catherine complained to John when Hazel happily organized her new room.

She stood outside Hazel's new chamber, protesting a father's acknowledgment of his illegitimate child. Her husband was to maintain racial boundaries, not blur them. Since Rosalind's mother was a slave, she became chattel under the doctrine *partus sequitur ventrem*. Yet even John Brower hesitated to bind her to base servitude, wishing to raise her with grace.

"I oversee dis' plantation. I'm their rightful owner. The option to have Hazel and Rosalind in dis' house is mine and mine alone," John argued.

"That's not true. I own most of the slaves and I'm your business partner at Rutherford Rocks. You don't do everything. You're in charge of the field slaves. I run this house, plan the meals, and—"

"I don't has time to argue wit' you. Give Hazel your old clothes or I's pick some out and do it myself."

Catherine propped her hands on her hips. "Why should a slave get to wear my clothes?"

"If yous don' want ta do it this way, I have to pay for a seamstress to make da clothes made for your lady's maid who livin' in this house. She gon' need better shoes, too. Take care of things or I will."

"I don't want her dressing me, doing my hair, and helping me around the house."

"Did yous hear anything I said? It's my decision ta make."

"Are you finished?"

"If there is nothing else that you would like to discuss wit' me, leave."

"I hate you, John!"

"You rant and talk nonstop. Yous do not have da upper hand. No woman does."

Hazel chuckled, settling onto her new bed.

Standing in the next room, overhearing everything, Hazel giggled. "He mines now, Missus. I love 'em!"

Overhearing Hazel, Catherine stormed into the room. "What did you say?"

"Nuthin', Missus."

"I heard every word. Stop coming after a married man."

"Well, I hope you heard da part 'bout Massa coming after me first, 'cause you don't own him. He do what he want ta do and I's gots ta lissen."

Catherine moved to strike Hazel, but John stayed her hand. "Marking and whipping our slaves makes them hard to sell. Don't cha' mess up Hazel's skin."

"You never want Hazel to be whipped or hit for anything!"

Hazel smiled. She knew Massa Brower's protection stemmed from affection. "Yous don't whip me 'cause yous a sweet and soft woman."

"I'm the one who owns you."

"It don't counts for nuttin' at Rutherford Rocks. Yo' husband gives da slaves instruction."

When Catherine withdrew, flushed with anger, even Hazel recognized Massa Brower's perverse attachment. She took pleasure in Catherine's questioned femininity, for Massa Brower had no desire for a wife who assumed masculine authority. Catherine mourned anew that Henry's sale had left Hazel unattached, allowing her husband's attention to settle where it ought not. Had she insisted Henry remain, perhaps John's eye would not have wandered.

Catherine could not undo Henry's sale, the one man who might have kept Hazel's loyalty. She seized their wedding portrait from the mantle, tore it from its frame, and shredded it to pieces. Thus did her life continue to unravel, one misfortune following another.

5

Women at War

❧⟫⟫⟩⟨⟨⟨❧

Catherine's subsequent attempts at motherhood ended in miscarriage and wounded pride. Yet Hazel conceived again. She ceased resisting Brower's advances upon realizing the privileges that accompanied her position as plantation mistress. While other parents toiled in the fields and dwelled in crude log cabins with earthen floors, Rosalind and Hazel enjoyed the comforts of the Great House, never again to sleep upon straw. Given lighter duties away from Alabama's scorching fields, Hazel became an informant against disobedient slaves.

Hazel bore a son, Bradley, securing Massa Brower's legacy from the auction block. Though other slave children mocked their elevated status, Brower's heart had softened, granting them finer food and clothing, lighter duties, and his particular favor.

His gentle caresses of Hazel's face seemed to beg silent forgiveness for his initial violations, though no formal apology passed his lips.

Upon returning from church, Catherine discovered Hazel and Rosalind partaking of flapjacks, a fare reserved for the master's table.

"The better job ya do, the more privileges you get," Massa Brower told Rosalind.

Yet Rosalind performed little labor in the Great House. She scorned such tasks as wiping crumbs from tablecloths or maintaining the grounds. Instead, she passed her hours with marbles and dolls and was granted daily instruction in letters and numbers while other enslaved children hauled water to the fields. No lash had ever marked her flesh. When taunted by her peers, she grew bold.

"Look at me. Who you think my pappy is?"

"Shush, gal!" Hazel said to quiet her.

"Everyone knows it," Rosalind proclaimed.

Whispers rippled through the church pews regarding Brower's slave mistress bearing a third child.

"There's already one of those high yellow-looking ones that has his same face. I guess more embarrassment makes no difference to Brower," a woman said, fanning herself in a pew.

"Poor Catherine. She must be devastated by the news that her husband has impregnated a nigger again," another woman whispered.

The women cast knowing glances at Catherine, who maintained her composure while feigning deafness to their words. Though uncertain of these fresh rumors, she knew well that her husband had gained his desired son. Each moment brought dual heartbreak—pain and shame intermingled. Catherine harbored fears that Bradley might somehow inherit Rutherford Rocks, despite present laws forbidding such.

Catherine pressed her palms together while talking to God. "What about me? Do my prayers count to God's ears?"

Her prayers for fertility remained unanswered while the plantation prospered. Catherine hardened herself, continuing to trade in human flesh—separating mothers, sons, daughters, and fathers when profit beckoned. She orchestrated forced breeding between strong slaves and compelled young girls to physically chastise their mothers for infractions. Few boundaries remained sacred in her pursuit of wealth through bondage. The Mississippi Married Women's Property Law of 1839 permitted her ownership of slaves, as did similar statutes in other states. She favored purchasing women with children, knowing a fertile mother increased her wealth.

As Catherine's reputation for brutality and wealth grew throughout Alabama, her social standing rose while she withdrew from society. Her genteel pastimes gave way to strong drink and tyrannical outbursts.

Catherine was surprised but elated that her sister, Sarah Ann, paid her a visit at Rutherford Rocks.

"I've lost track of time," said Catherine.

"I hadn't. It's been two whole years since I've seen you face-to-face. Moving to Massachusetts has made travel so much more challenging," Sarah Ann replied.

During Sarah Ann's visit, the sisters walked the garden discussing Catherine's deepening involvement in slavery.

"When Daddy died, I sold my last slave. I realized how wrong it was to mistreat humans. You really should think more about your Christian values. It's time to dig deeper to create a systematic change. It is unrighteous to rely on someone else's labor and benefit from slavery," Sarah Ann said.

Sarah Ann, being brotherless like Catherine, inherited less property and chattel. Catherine's marriage secured her the greater portion of the wealth.

"Everything I learned about slavery, I learned from our parents."

"That doesn't make it right."

"We grew up going to slave auctions. They waited on you before you could even talk. You're a White, Southern woman with privileges. Now you feel guilty about the way niggers have been treated?"

"Don't call them niggers!" Sarah Ann raised her voice.

The sisters halted near the cotton field. Catherine summoned a child laboring among the weeds.

"You ate one of my biscuits, didn't you?"

"Yee, yeehs," the little boy said, stuttering.

"Hold out your hand," Catherine ordered. As the boy did, she swatted his hand with a whip. Blood coursed down the child's hands from Catherine's blows. "That's for forgetting to call me what you should've!"

"Missus! Missus!" the boy called out.

Though he had once forgotten the title drilled into him since age four, Catherine showed no mercy. The cook had offered him mere scraps—a sliver of ham and a discarded biscuit. His father tended the plantation's livestock, while the enslaved subsisted on cast-off parts—chitterlings, fatty cuts, pig's feet. Children ate their corn mush from trays laid on the ground.

"If you ever steal food from me again, I'll sell you. You'll never see your mother and father again. Get back to work!"

The child fled to the cotton rows, disappearing under his mother's worried gaze.

Sarah Ann frowned at her sister. "He can't be more than five years old. You're a monster in the making. It's a sin to treat a child harshly this way."

"It's no different than poking a pig with a stick. I've made him come to the Great House and dance to entertain at one of my parties. The little darkie understands my expectations. If he does better and stops making excuses for not doing what he's supposed to do, I'll treat him to a piece of candy when he comes back to dance."

Sarah Ann gasped. "How could you say and do such evil things to a child? You don't even act humane anymore?"

"You grew up owning and beating slaves yourself. Don't act like you've never struck one."

"I know better, so I must do better. Slavery is going to bring this country to its knees. God will not reward the sin of slavery. Don't you want to go to Heaven someday?"

"Slavery isn't that serious. Even George Washington owned slaves. His wife, Martha, did, too. I don't know what's gotten into you. If I accidentally kill one of these little slaves, I'm covered by the Casual Killing Act."

"You don't have one compassionate bone left in your body, do you?"

"Where is my sister who was born and raised in the South?"

"I'll regard that question as a compliment from someone like you."

"You're too humble and unassuming. I guess that's why you don't have a good Southern husband. None of the eligible bachelors want you, Sarah Ann." Catherine smiled.

"I labor for our Master. I want to save this country more than I care about marriage."

Catherine clapped. "What a liberated woman."

"This will be my last time setting foot on Rutherford Rocks land so long as you are living so ungodly."

"Since we're so divided on this issue, I won't miss you for one second in this lifetime."

"We all are God's children. You will be held accountable by the good Lord one day if you don't stop what you're doing."

"If I didn't know better, I would think my sister is turning into an abolitionist."

"That, I proudly am!" Sarah Ann headed for a horse-drawn carriage.

"Stay in the North with your kind. Long live the confederacy!"

Sarah Ann turned a final time, shaking her head. She had freed her hundred slaves in Massachusetts with papers of manumission, though she spoke not of it. The law forbade freed Blacks from remaining in Alabama beyond thirty days after Nat Turner's uprising in Virginia.

Sarah Ann drew inspiration from Robert Carter III, who had liberated more than five hundred souls in 1791 following his conversion to the Baptist faith—the largest emancipation before 1860. Whispers held that "Black Brother Will" was Carter's half-brother, born of Robert II and an enslaved woman. Though Carter owned his own brother, he worked within the law's constraints to free his chattels.

Sarah Ann labored quietly in the abolitionist cause, despising bondage as her sister remained ignorant of her convictions.

"You may be my blood relative, but you're a plumb fool," Catherine called after her departed sister.

Catherine stalked the grounds, berating slaves for the slightest infractions before retreating to the coolness of the Great House. Within, Hazel had swept, dusted, and polished the furnishings. While Hazel gathered fresh linens, Catherine noticed her swelling belly and struck the sheets from her hands.

"I's got to freshen up your sheets before your hot supper is ready."

"I don't want them! Do the task I gave you to do. You don't listen to me anymore!" Catherine lunged toward Hazel.

Hazel struggled to bend over to pick up the linen. "What's wrong with you, Missus?"

Catherine multiplied Hazel's duties before any could be completed.

"What do you think's wrong with me? Keep your hands off my husband. I don't need this stress. You keep bothering him. Do your work. Focus on what you should!" Catherine shouted, with trembling hands.

"I's sorry but I don't look for him. Massa Brower comes ta me. Talk to him 'bout his ways."

Hazel's speech had grown refined since moving to the Great House, her appearance more genteel. Massa Brower's gifts and privileges had granted her an unseemly dignity.

"Hazel, you've changed. You're not who I thought you were when I was a little girl," Catherine said, vexation rising.

"Those who do the most complain the least. I'm the one who keeps this house spotless. Your job is to put clothes and shoes on the slave's back and feet and get help for the sick, but you don't do it much for people who give you the life of leisure, Missus."

"You think you're so smart. You and your slave children are intolerable. I own all of you!"

"Yes, the devil does own us. You nothing but the nastiest White woman in all of Alabama."

"You're not even a human being! The law agrees!" Catherine yelled.

"You knew your husband's character before he laid eyes on me. You ain't deaf or dumb, Missus. He touched too many of us in his big old feather bed, in the garden, or anywhere. You don't own enough eyes to keep the man's feet still."

Catherine brandished a hickory switch, lashing Hazel with masculine strength.

"You whipped me so much it don't hurt my flesh no more. Make it fall off me bones if ya want to."

"You have too much courage to speak to me this way after my parents put a roof over your head and food in your little mouth when you were a little girl. How ungrateful could you be?" Catherine dropped the switch, seizing Hazel's throat. "You're nothing but a servant who will never amount to anything!"

Hazel's screams brought Massa Brower running.

"Get your hands off Hazel!" Massa Brower restrained Catherine with contempt. "I told you to leave her alone. Don't ever punish her. I'll take care of that."

"And I told you to stop sleeping with that trashy bed wench and making little niggers. Did you, though? Instead, you made more! Tell me something, John. Is it true that a third one is on the way?"

"Don't matter. You won't have my children. If you were my very choice to marry, we should have at least one son to inherit this plantation."

He considered Hazel's sturdy form against Catherine's indolent ways, watching slave girls fan her with peacock feathers while she could not bear even one child. He no longer shared Catherine's chamber; her complaints of his snoring had driven him away. Hazel received him as though with love, no longer resisting his advances, having learned to return his kisses.

"I don't have control over my body. I want to have children! How is this my fault?"

"If you have a debt that you can't pay, that's not my fault either. I'll do what I want with my slaves, my wife, or anyone else. You just a woman. Don't question my actions."

"I hate you!" Catherine fled to their bedroom.

"I'm not exactly your biggest fan, my dear. Our relationship is strictly business. I'm the owner of dis great, big, wonderful plantation. You don't even do ya' job to manage it properly." Massa Brower followed her.

Catherine harbored secrets of her own—carefully crafted baby clothes stored away for her future children. She remained determined that Providence would grant her unexpected fertility, coveting Hazel's fecundity while plotting to secure heirs of her own for Rutherford Rocks.

"Whatever are you talking about? Rutherford Rocks has increased in profitability tenfold. We are now in the position to buy a second plantation."

"Now that we have two men running it, I guess ya right," John said.

"What is that supposed to mean?"

"You used to be a soft, polished, subservient Southern woman," John said as twilight dimmed the window.

"And you didn't always socialize with our slaves."

"If ya mean Hazel and her children, they are only here for benevolent purposes."

"You've got to make every one of them do right if you want a desired result. No revolution remains bloodless." Catherine lit a candle.

She stifled words about his paternal instincts driving Hazel's elevation. Instead, she sought healing by extending her hand to John. Her bitter, deep-seated ill will dissolved in the candlelight when he drew her close. Her hopes quickened at the prospect of a long-awaited kiss. Despite her trials, she refused to surrender. John's demeanor softened at her show of tenderness.

"Thank you," Catherine said after John's gentle kiss.

She lay back, listening to the rain as it fell, nature's music soothing her troubled mind. In rare tenderness, they found momentary peace. More kisses followed as vulnerability replaced their hardened hearts.

"I've missed you. I'm sorry for not being an example of Christian love. Do you still love me, John?"

John valued his wife's gratitude and desire. He felt a familiar stirring, half-inclined to resume his role as protector.

John's silence spoke volumes. His marriage to Catherine had been one of convenience, the Marshalls' wealth his true objective. He had deceived them about his assets.

Known for their cunning and strategy, the Browers were secretly indebted to many. John had never desired marriage, but knew a Marshall union would ease his path. Catherine's mother's connections to Tinsdale University, with its profitable use of slave labor, had proved invaluable.

Catherine ignored John's greater interest in cotton prices than her affection. A tear traced her cheek as she hoped their barrier might dissolve. Their shared caresses offered some relief from her suffering.

"I still have faith that you do love me," Catherine told John, drawing closer. Pride swelled at her restraint of hatred, despite his torments. She embraced him as on their wedding night. "Yesterday is behind us."

"Whenever you show up like this, we won' argue," John whispered.

"You'll always be my husband."

John had no intention of departure—their legal arrangements prevented Catherine from relinquishing control. Though he could manage her assets, they remained legally hers, a deliberate move by the Marshalls. John required Catherine's position to maintain his desired lifestyle. Remembering her worth, he kissed her softly while thinking of Hazel. Both women served his purposes.

"You always gon' be my wife. I love ya." John knew that was a lie.

Catherine embraced him, relief flooding her heart. At last, she felt superior to Hazel. Her contentment lasted only until a piercing scream split the air. Startled, John sprang up and gathered his clothes.

The overseer entered the room. "I's sorry ta bother ya. There's trouble with one of the slaves."

And thus was Catherine nearly broken beyond repair.

6

Aunt Sarah: Friend, Protector, Soul Food Cuisine Originator

Mumbling, Aunt Sarah held a small knife in her hand. "Lawd hab mercy, mah po' back achin' from all dis work. I don't git nary a minute ta rest mahself."

The stout plantation cook suppressed her tears while peeling potatoes, a hot breeze caressing her arms. Though she maintained the demeanor of a willing servant, her heart bore equal measures of love and sorrow. While other slaves enjoyed their Sabbath rest, her labors continued without ceasing. The kitchen stood separate from the Great House as protection against fire, and being quartered there meant Aunt Sarah could neither escape her duties nor prepare meals in advance. Catherine demanded all dishes be fresh, hot, and perfectly seasoned.

Rhodie, one of her assistant cooks, shook her head. "Tain't nothin' compared to what dem field hands sufferin' through, day in and day out. Dey gits de whup and ain't got a blessed thing in dem quarters. Dem others would thank de Good Lawd to have what you got. Us youngins out here ain't even got shoes nor rags to cover ourselves."

Rhodie had begun as a weed-puller before Massa Brower noted her intelligence and placed her in the kitchen. Aunt Sarah's age prevented fieldwork now, though she had known such labor as a child after captivity in a cell at Gorée Island off Senegal's coast with her young sister. The girls had passed through the "Door of No Return" on that forty-five-acre island, their last departure point before the months-long Atlantic crossing. Aunt Sarah's sister perished near the journey's end in the New World.

Aunt Sarah had maintained a gentle, docile nature despite never reuniting with her family. Sold to Catherine's family, she had raised Catherine and Sarah Ann as a devoted mammy, nursing them alongside her own infant son. Her boy grew tall but lean, forever yearning for his mother's attention. Catherine had not recognized Aunt Sarah's other talents until observing her nurturing ways with her son and the other slave children. Aunt Sarah later instructed Catherine and Sarah Ann in respect, quilting and sewing, enhancing their worth as young ladies. She played marbles with them, sang children's songs, and taught moral lessons while her son, Warren, toiled in the fields from dawn to dusk after turning eight.

Sarah Ann held a particular fondness for Aunt Sarah. Catherine's jealousy of Warren emerged when she informed her father of his attempts at literacy.

"Massa Johnson, I's down on mah knees beggin' ya, please don't sell mah boy chile," Aunt Sarah pleaded with tears in her eyes. Trained never to meet a White person's gaze, she lowered her head in shame.

"I can't make no money off disobedient chilluns."

"Lawd knows he jes' copyin' what he see Miss Catherine and Miss Ann do wit' dem books, Massa. He ain't nuthin' but playin' like de chillun do. Mah Warren don't know how ta read no words. No, suh."

Massa Johnson held up a book Warren had taken. "He knows that slaves can't learn nothin'!"

Warren clung to his mother's skirt, crying out and wetting himself when torn from her embrace. His twin had died at birth.

Aunt Sarah could only entreat Providence that her sole surviving son might grow to manhood. The incident awakened Sarah Ann to slavery's cruelties while emboldening Catherine. Aunt Sarah returned to fieldwork when the girls matured, until Massa Johnson learned of the slaves' praise for her cornbread and venison, even with meager provisions in their cabins. The field hands spoke of her cooking while working with the mules, eagerly anticipating her meals. They willingly hunted game for her kitchen, grateful for her skill in preparation.

She wed twice more, bearing eight children after Warren, including several sets of twins. The Johnsons had sold them all, save the three youngest who remained at Rutherford Rocks. Aunt Sarah's husband perished while chopping wood for the Great House's furnishings. "De Lawd done give ya yo' final rest, de only peace we po' souls ever knows," Aunt Sarah had said, pressing her lips to his for the final time.

Her remaining children labored in the fields while she managed the kitchen staff, ensuring the perfect execution of every dish. Though she took pride in preventing errors that might bring punishment, the constant vigilance drained her spirit and body. None who gazed upon Aunt Sarah's reddened eyes perceived her exhaustion at sixty-five years. She was remarkable for having no major ailments, as most slaves perished before their fourth decade.

Her long life had brought little joy. Grief and anxiety were luxuries she could not afford while preparing roasted beef, puddings, jellies, slow-cooked meats, oyster stews, sweet potato pies, ice cream, and seasonal fish from scratch, while managing imported spices. Her knowledge of West African dishes with okra and rice enhanced the exotic menus served to elite guests who came to enjoy Rutherford Rocks' wine, grand meals, and Southern hospitality.

Known for her vibrant-colored head wraps and mastery of deep-fried fish, black-eyed peas, and countless other dishes, not once did Aunt Sarah burn a biscuit, though maintaining such vigilance meant sleeping in the kitchen yard. She provided comfort to all who crossed the threshold, a hospitable presence serving both guests and the master's family.

"I's git scraps and leavin's. Ain't 'lowed ta taste nary a morsel of what I fixes fo' de White folks at dey table."

"Po' souls in de field gotta slip food in dey pockets when dey ain't got nuthin' to fill dey bellies wit'," Rhodie reasoned.

"But lissen to dat." She overheard guests praising her cooking, though none would grant her the title of chef.

"This food is outstanding, Catherine. I've never tasted roasted chicken quite like it! Who made this exquisite meal?"

"I'm so pleased that you like it. It's just a little something I put together from family recipes." Catherine's tongue spewed the biggest lie.

"Your Negroes don't cook?" a woman asked.

"They don't have much sense, especially the oldest one who can't follow directions on her own. All she wants to do is eat and sleep. She even hides in the closet, so she doesn't have to lift her finger. When she does cooperate, I must give her specific instructions about how to measure and prepare the ingredients."

"That must be exhausting. Why do you put up with her?"

"She's old and rather thick-headed. I feel sorry for Aunt Sarah. Who would want to buy her?"

"I had one of those. She ate more than she worked and wasn't worth the price I paid for her," another female slave owner added.

The woman dropped her dinner napkin. A small child darted forward to retrieve it. Another youth appeared to fan away the flies as they emerged.

"You're so good to your slaves. Helping in the kitchen is too much work. I would've taught her a lesson by now.

Reestablish your authority. Those mulattoes are usually smarter. Let her train one of them and give her something else to do," the first woman said.

Catherine smiled. "I do aim to please my guests, so I didn't mind overseeing things to ensure that everything would be done properly for my dearest friends today."

A tear traced Aunt Sarah's cheek. "Ev'rybody on dis plantation know Aunt Sarah cook de finest vittles dey ever put in dey mouths. Missus ain't neva touched a pot nor pan. I's de one dat showed her ev'rything she know 'bout cookin', but she don't tell nobody dat. Miss Catherine don't care if I works 'til mah po' feet give out," she mumbled, her pride wounded.

She had carried food to the dining room, glimpsing the high-society guests, savoring her carefully prepared feast with silver utensils. The sight of genteel Southern ladies in their crinoline-supported gowns reminded her that the most refined appearance often masked the greatest brutality.

Though Aunt Sarah required no physical coercion to maintain discipline and had never felt the lash, her spirit bore deep scars. When carrying dishes from the detached kitchen to the main house, she had to whistle nonstop to prove she neither sampled nor sullied the food, though Catherine dismissed this as mere folklore.

Rhodie sucked her teeth. "Aunt Sarah, who you done gone and got yo'self thinkin' you is? You jes' a colored woman in de White folks' house, ain't no fine lady, ain't no special guest, ain't nobody dat matters to dem."

"You best mind yo' place and keep outta mah business, chile. Aunt Sarah been fixin' fancy vittles fo' de massa's family longer den you been drawin' breath on dis earth. You ain't old enough ta know 'bout such things, no suh."

Hazel's arrival interrupted their private exchange. Aunt Sarah cleared her throat, warning Rhodie. "Hazel's comin'." Both fell silent as footsteps approached.

Aunt Sarah harbored contempt for Hazel and her children, who enjoyed the privileges of literacy, self-advocacy, and comfortable beds. Rhodie shared her mistrust of those who escaped Massa Brower's usual harsh treatment.

"We don' like dem. They don' like us," she said, convincing Rhodie.

The mistress still slept while Hazel completed her washing and ironing. Hazel commanded no loyalty in their world. Aunt Sarah, Rhodie, and the others often communicated through spirituals to convey hidden messages. They never sang these songs in the presence of Hazel and her children, whom they mistrusted. Awaiting her words, they maintained their distance.

Hazel stood in the doorway. "I'm lookin' for Mistress Catherine."

"She ain't in here. Best look yonder in de barn or out wit' dem field hands," Aunt Sarah snapped, grasping an iron skillet.

Hazel examined Aunt Sarah from head to toe." Do you have a problem with me?"

"Nobody say dat. Don't make up anything to carries back to Massa 'bout me being sassy, ya hear?"

Aunt Sarah longed to denounce Hazel as an affront to hardworking slave women. Though fully Negro, Hazel carried herself as one employed by Whites rather than enslaved by them. She affected refined tastes, wrapping herself in cast-off silks as though her greatest burden was leisurely repose beneath a shady tree. Her sole accomplishment was bearing the master's children while the Browers amassed generational wealth.

"De black walnut bread ready, Aunt Sarah," Rhodie said, breaking the tense silence.

Aunt Sarah took comfort that Rhodie had escaped fieldwork. The girl's heaviest task was carrying water to the field hands. At merely nine years old, she had mastered bread-baking before dawn.

That night, Aunt Sarah's arthritic hands ached from slicing meat. Her feet throbbed from standing throughout the day in deteriorating shoes. Dizziness from hunger overcame her. Though she nourished so many, she had never tasted her own peach cobbler. Her thoughts turned to her children at the plantation and to Rhodie, still with her mother. Recent years had worn her spirit thin, though none took notice. The sight of Hazel's privileges pained her. Managing the kitchen without recognition had become an endless battle.

None perceived her cracking fingernails from poor nourishment or the toll of ill-treatment. Though she remained nurturing and capable, her age rendered her invisible. She took pride in satisfying all who ate her food. She had even aided Catherine's quest for fertility, their lives entwined. She viewed Catherine as a granddaughter, praying on her knees while holding Catherine's hands.

"A miracle is on da way," Aunt Sarah had told Catherine.

She had crafted herbal remedies, hoping to resolve Catherine's barrenness.

Though Sarah Ann had sworn never to return while slavery persisted at Rutherford Rocks, her abolitionist work drew her back. She feigned reconciliation with her sister as a strategy, coming for Aunt Sarah's sake with news of Warren. When Catherine and Massa Brower were absent, the women spoke candidly.

"I had to come back to check on you. You're like a second mother to me. I never liked the way you've been treated by my family." Sarah Ann embraced Aunt Sarah, sharing a rare moment of confession to an enslaved woman about her rejection of slavery. She perceived the cook's inner decay.

"I best gets back to my cookin'. I gots to do it six times a day."

"You can talk to me, Aunt Sarah." She gently gripped the sides of her shoulders.

"I wish I had da time. I don' wan' get whupped."

"I'll make sure that doesn't happen. Human beings don't deserve to get hit."

"Ain't nobody neva looked on me wit' no kindness. Can't call nuthin' my own 'cause I's jes' property. My heart still bleedin' from when dey took my firstborn chile."

"I heard where Warren is. That's what I wanted to tell you in confidence."

Aunt Sarah's face brightened. "What? He okay? He alive?"
"Yes."

Aunt Sarah beseeched Providence for deliverance. In her mind's eye, she glimpsed an open door. Freedom beckoned, promising escape from victimhood. Sarah Ann then revealed her own path.

"I'm involved in the Underground Railroad. I've been helping slaves escape. I'm an abolitionist. I want slavery to stop."

Bewilderment crossed Aunt Sarah's features at Sarah Ann's compassion. Her upbringing had taught her that Whites and Blacks could never share a common cause.

"But I's property."

"I see you and this world differently. We should leave this world behind and put a new one together."

"Who gonna trouble deyself wit' a wore-out ole colored woman? Ain't worth nuthin' but fifty dollas now dat dese bones is gettin' old and tired."

"You're a human being, and you're the best cook in the state of Alabama. I should say chef."

Joy illuminated Aunt Sarah's countenance at the title.

"I remember the way you used to let me and Catherine lick the spoons when you were baking one of your famous cakes." Sarah Ann smiled. "Oh, how I liked the taste of the batter even before the cake was ready."

"You liked my bakin' dat much?"

"Your baking, your cooking, and your love. You taught me to give compliments freely. Spending time with you made a big difference in my life."

"I's did all dat for you?" Aunt Sarah raised her eyebrows.

"Yes! You did!" Sarah Ann joyfully clasped her hands.

Aunt Sarah marveled at such freely given praise. Her recognition of her gifts strengthened her resolve and heightened her yearning for freedom. Trust bloomed between them swiftly.

"You sees me like I's a real person?"

"Do you know we were named after the same person? My grandmother. I know your life hasn't been rosy. You've been forced to behave as if your suffering hasn't been cruel. Imagine running north and finally being free with Warren." Sarah Ann clasped her hands.

Their exchange laid bare every transgression between enslaved and enslaver. The rising price of slaves, driven by import restrictions and the abolitionist movement, had disrupted the Southern economy. Yet Sarah Ann sought moral redemption for her past ownership of human beings. She and Aunt Sarah crafted plans for reunion with Warren. Sarah Ann wished to give Aunt Sarah the chance to know peace.

"I want to give you the gift of freedom." Sarah Ann planted the seed.

"Da good Lawd done touched yo' heart somethin' special, wantin' ta end dis sufferin'."

"I can't fix everything, but I'd like to start by helping someone who has always been there for me. I didn't forget how you took up for me when Catherine tried to get me in trouble. You taught me about loyalty."

She still treasured the quilt Aunt Sarah had sewn her by hand. Sarah Ann's own mother had shown her little tenderness or care.

"You mean so much to me." Sarah Ann covered her face with her hands. "You deserve a better life."

"It be okay, Missus." Aunt Sarah held Sarah Ann's hand. "S'pose somebody see me and ask where I's goin'? Massa's men gon' beat dis ol' body sumthin' terrible if dey cotch me runnin'. Don't want no price on my head, no suh."

"There's no Underground Railroad in Alabama. I can't guarantee you anything, but the choice is yours."

Aunt Sarah's defenses melted as trust deepened. She released Sarah Ann's hand to embrace her, gently rubbing her back as she had done in Sarah Ann's childhood.

"Look—there's a risk that I could be murdered if anyone finds out that I'm against slavery and that I'm helping you. I drank milk from your breasts. I can only tell you that I'll help you to be careful. We both have something to lose. I love you so much."

"I loves you somethin' fierce, Missus. You always been de kindest one of dem sisters, sweet as honey. You's like my own chile, dat's what you is to me."

After Aunt Sarah opened her heart to Sarah Ann, they settled upon a plan. After preparing the hoecake batter for the morning's breakfast, she would place black pepper in her shoes before taking flight. Should bloodhounds pursue, they would lose her scent. She must cross the swampy river, board a steamboat to Mobile, then seek a wagon for passage.

I's near 'bout forgot mah walkin' stick, she thought, grasping the carved wood.

Hope lent strength to Aunt Sarah's limbs as she crept away from Rutherford Rocks in darkness, walking stick firmly in her right hand. When she reached the edge of the property, she broke into as swift a run as her legs could manage. The promise of reuniting with Warren sustained her as she pressed on toward freedom.

7

Pushed to the Edge

◦❯❯❯❮❮❮◦

On a moonlit night, two events transpired. Hazel birthed a boy named Bradley—news unknown to Catherine. The mistress, wrapped in her comfortable robe, gathered the first group of house servants. Massa Brower joined them in the parlor after viewing his firstborn son, whereupon the overseer delivered troubling news.

"Aunt Sarah ran off." Jake, tall and lanky with weeks of stubble, blinked nervously with bloodshot eyes, worry evident in his manner.

"Why would Aunt Sarah run off? She loves me, and she was greatly beloved. And why would she leave her kids?" Catherine paced.

"I checked every cabin and every inch of Rutherford Rocks. I even checked the boards in da ceiling. The only thing I could find was a few barefoot tracks."

Catherine scanned the assembled servants. "Has anyone seen Aunt Sarah?"

She approached Rhodie and Aunt Sarah's children—Bessie, Wiley, and Polly—holding a brass lamp aloft to study their expressions before placing it on a table.

"Not you, you, you, or even you?" she asked, jabbing each chest with her finger.

"No, Missus," they responded in sorrowful succession.

Catherine slouched. "This makes no sense. I didn't give her a pass to leave the plantation. She's simply not late coming back."

The overseer stood with his hands on his hips. "I went as far as twenty miles out. Aunt Sarah ain't nowhere close to these parts."

Catherine shook her head. "Somebody is lying. A slave I've given the best of everything to can't just vanish into thin air. Aunt Sarah is owned by good Southern people."

Catherine felt betrayed. Just as she and her husband attempted to rekindle their bond, slave catchers prowled the neighboring woods in search of Aunt Sarah. Catherine dispatched her fiercest bloodhound to the hunt. Her mind raced with possibilities. A reward might prove necessary. She dreaded the thought of Aunt Sarah being sold at a public auction.

"I only trust Aunt Sarah to routinely prepare and oversee my food. No one else but my pet Negro. And who is going to make sure the vegetables in the garden grow?" With tears, Catherine complained to Massa Brower.

The memory of Aunt Sarah's perfectly seasoned vegetables, their aroma filling the air from the iron pots, haunted her.

"There's nothin' more that can be done tonight. We must wait," Massa Brower announced.

"How could you be so calm? Aunt Sarah's the head cook. She keeps our family going. Our guests look forward to special occasions at Rutherford Rocks because Aunt Sarah—"

Massa Brower cut off his agitated wife. "Catherine, get ya' mind together. Everything that can be done at this hour has been. I don' know what you expect to happen. Do ya think Aunt Sarah will suddenly just show up?"

"She might. Maybe someone kidnapped her."

"Lissen to me; Aunt Sarah is a strong, wrinkled up old Black woman. Who would want her? We don' know anything."

"Aunt Sarah has the most familiarity with the crops that are grown at Rutherford Rocks, and she shapes plantation cuisine."

"Why don't you put your trust in God by praying for Aunt Sarah's safe return? He makes ways to receive answers."

Catherine attempted prayer, silently beseeching the Lord to return her property. "Lord, we put our trust in You. May Your hand be on this confusing situation," Hazel cried out, interrupting.

Having given birth before, she had returned to her duties as always. She had left her newborn with the midwife when Jake summoned her. Catherine's prayers ceased at the sound of that familiar voice. She who had elevated Hazel from a dirt floor crawling with vermin never imagined Aunt Sarah's discontent with bondage. In Catherine's mind, Aunt Sarah had been a contented mammy with no desire to improve her station.

Catherine peered at Hazel, lashing out. "I know you had something to do with this foolishness! My faithful servant loves me. She loves her job. What did you do to entice her to run away?"

The overseer scratched his ear, still blinking rapidly, pondering Aunt Sarah's whereabouts. He reported that she had bid farewell to her assistant after the evening's dishes were washed and the fire banked.

"None of this makes sense. Surely, you must have told her to do something like this. I never lost one slave," Catherine said to Hazel.

"Blame is the unhealthiest thing you can choose, Missus. Maybe you don' do as good of a job managing us as you think. Has it ever crossed ya' mind that problem's you?"

Hazel kissed Rosalind's head, then cast a brazen wink at Massa Brower, smiling. It was her signal for his company with her and the newborn.

"That's my husband!"

Hazel paused briefly. "I never said he wasn't. I know you're upset about Aunt Sarah. Would you like me to make a cup of tea for you or perhaps a drink?"

"No, I wouldn't."

Catherine struggled to master herself. The other slaves began to murmur and frown. None could fathom how she had allowed Hazel such power to disrupt the plantation's order.

Catherine withered like a parched vine. Her whip slipped from nerveless fingers, her brutality's glory fleeing. She approached her husband, seeking solace in her brokenness. He thrust her away with powerful hands, indifferent to her tears and loyalty.

"Don't touch me. You drove Hazel away being too brutal. Look what you've done," he told her, rejecting their marital bond.

"I didn't do anything."

Massa Brower shook his head. "Everyone *leave!*" he told the slaves.

Hazel lit his pipe without being bidden.

"I 'preciate you, Hazel. Go rest now."

Catherine sighed.

"If trouble might come, ya should always be ready for it," Massa Brower told his wife.

"Don't correct me in front of her." Catherine pointed to Hazel.

"I'll be waiting up for you, Massa," Hazel said.

Catherine's eyes narrowed to slits. Despair and offense warred within her. Though she recognized John Brower's legal authority over her as property, her heart ached at her powerlessness. She maintained a gentle facade as Hazel and Rosalind withdrew, though her wounds deepened. She sensed Hazel would continue to plague her peace.

Before Aunt Sarah's flight, she had restored Catherine's fertility through herbal remedies. Catherine had quietly transgressed to disrupt her abusive bond with Massa Brower. Providence had opened its floodgates—she carried a child, though not by a White man.

8

Set Up

❖⟫⟫❯❮❮❮❖

Catherine remained ignorant that Aunt Sarah's father had been a voodoo priest from West Africa. Aunt Sarah described her mystical abilities as those of a slave healer who could guide Catherine toward knowledge and a more prosperous life. She knew to guard certain truths about African religion. Another slave had informed her of Virginia's 1748 law forbidding enslaved people from preparing or administering medicine. Yet Catherine sought her aid without fear of poisoning, whether through potions or herbal applications to her skin.

"De trouble ain't what you reckon it is. Things gonna turn themselves 'round. A chile gon' come to ya soon," Aunt Sarah had told Catherine.

Though enslaved people had been Christianized, Aunt Sarah's first faith was not Christianity. She posed a hidden threat. Repression drove her to the ritual practices she had witnessed in Africa during Sunday ceremonies as a child. She employed these arts only to counter the evil of her foes.

Beneath the slave quarter's floor, she concealed talismans—necklaces, doll parts, bird skulls, roots, and seeds. Her prayers sought to sever Catherine's bond with Massa Brower and unite her with another man through conception. She beseeched forces from the depths to cloud Catherine's judgment. Aunt Sarah fashioned a voodoo doll to support her acts of secret resistance and spiritual warfare to alter Catherine's disposition.

Sarah Ann arrived after Aunt Sarah had begun her conjuring work. Before her flight, Aunt Sarah's spells worked their effect—Catherine grew mysteriously distant from her marriage, harboring such resentment toward her husband that scandal held no fear. She felt herself an emotional prisoner. If her husband could wound her through procreation with slave women, she could ease her loneliness and sorrow by mimicking his predatory habits. Yet Catherine needed someone to blame for Aunt Sarah's disappearance. With her husband accusing her, she turned on the overseer.

"You're incompetent, purely incapable of learning plantation management. Aunt Sarah got away. I'm being held responsible for it."

"I's in charge of the field hands. Aunt Sarah ain't work under me."

"Slaves will get into mischief if you allow it. Clearly, all of them at Rutherford Rocks don't fear you. You're fired!"

"But—"

"Get out of here, Jake. Your services are no longer needed at Rutherford Rocks." Catherine flung her arm, shooing him away.

"I hope all ya Negroes leave and never come back dis' way!"

"Since you can't do the job you were hired to do, keep quiet, walk fast, and leave. I can't stand the sight of poor White trash."

Catherine resolved to try a new approach to replace Jake. After examining a man called Juniper, she purchased the large, muscular slave from the auction block. He had been bought and sold repeatedly, rented to numerous planters who used him as a breeder. Initially, Catherine intended him to sire children with the enslaved women at Rutherford Rocks, as his powerful build suggested he could easily manage heavy labor. More births meant more free labor for the vast plantation.

"Sold," Catherine told the auctioneer.

Yet she soon saw a different potential in Juniper. She appointed him as the slave driver to guard the plantation's economic interests.

"If you want privileges here, you must forget sympathy. Handle the whip better than Jake to make 'em work and behave," Catherine advised Juniper.

She had no intentions of having him whipped upon joining Rutherford Rocks. As she observed Juniper directing slaves in cotton picking, digging, and yard work, he became the object of her desire. His appeal grew irresistible the day he bound a field hand to a tree for working too slowly.

"When dat work bell sound dis mornin' fo' dawn, everybody done got here 'cept you draggin' along last as usual. You reckon dat's gonna make me praise ya?" Juniper told Rufus.

"I'm not gon work 'til I's fall out. I's gots to take my time. I's been sick."

"Don't you dare run yo' mouth at me dat way. You jes' playin' sick 'cause you too lazy to work."

"Look at dese hands, all raw and bleedin'. I been sick down in mah bones and ain't got no food in mah belly. Nothin' but some ol' peas and a piece of cornbread pass mah lips. Had ta give de last morsel to mah boy chile what's growin' and starvin'. I swear fo' de Lawd I's doin' all I got strength to do."

"Dat's all you got to give? Ain't worth de breath you wastin'. You jes' a no-account lazy nigger."

Rufus stood ramrod straight. "Ya can't break me, *nigger*."

Juniper stepped close to Rufus, and tilted his head. "I sho' can, and I's gonna work you 'til you de best field hand, or I's gonna see you sold right off dis plantation!" Juniper drew the coiled leather from his belt, letting it unfurl with a menacing hiss. The well-worn braided whip, dark with use and age, caught the sunlight as he gripped the smooth wooden handle. Dew still clung to the leather in the early morning air as he prepared to assert his authority.

After Juniper finished laying the hickory whip across Rufus's bare flesh, silence fell. Blood and tears mingled on the man's body.

Though Juniper and Rufus shared the same coal-black complexion, Juniper wielded authority to punish and lecture Rufus as though Providence had not made them equal. "One mo' cross word outta yo' mouth and I's gonna take a hot iron to yo' hide. Life and death at Rutherford Rocks is in my hands now."

Juniper maintained a closer watch over the slaves than Jake ever had, his surveillance relentless and precise. Though he drove them hard through the heat and dusk, he offered incentives for harder work—extra rations and clothing. However, Rufus found no contentment in unpaid toil. He resented being called lazy and had no wish to die enriching Massa Brower.

The hour had come for the slaves to eat and rest before morning's labors. After Rufus's young son finished tending the livestock, the concerned child rubbed fat meat across his father's back to ease the wounds. He prayed no large blisters would form. Nothing remained but to massage his father's swollen ankles and feet with horse liniment.

After the slaves had returned to their cabins, Catherine and John shared a moment in the parlor. Four months had passed without sight of Aunt Sarah. Catherine had expected her return by now. "If she's living, she'll show up when she gets hungry. She'll miss her days at Rutherford Rocks. Aunt Sarah isn't intelligent enough to know what to think or do much longer," Catherine told her husband, John.

John shook his head. "She hasn't been found dead in the woods, no bloodhounds caught hold of her, and no slave catcher came forward to collect a reward."

Catherine privately harbored fears of slave revolt, her anxiety heightened by Aunt Sarah's absence and a missing gun from her husband's collection.

♋

One day, unable to shake thoughts of Juniper's strong, protective arms, she drew him aside.

"Missus, I knows dis here's all business and I's tryin' to help you run it proper. Don't mean I's showin' favor to my own peoples. I knows who puts de food in my mouth."

Though Catherine desired Juniper to intimidate the slaves, she wished to avoid stirring collective bitterness or dampening morale. Yet she voiced no protest at his methods. Juniper's mastery of self-hatred shone brilliantly.

"I approve of your decision." Smiling, she regarded him with admiration.

At first, Catherine could only stare at Juniper. Though she attempted to look elsewhere, she couldn't stop staring at his skin, his eyes, his gait, his commanding presence. Mesmerized, she struggled to find words.

"We make a good team, don't we?"

"I reckon we does, Missus. I's jes' doin' what I's told to do."

"You've taught me to be less harsh and more efficient."

The day's labor had been demanding. Juniper, a man of few words, longed only to tend his vegetable garden and hunt rabbits or possums. His thoughts dwelled on sweet potatoes roasting in his cast iron Dutch oven. Yet, Catherine persisted in conversation until she reached to touch his lips with her fingertips.

Juniper flinched. I ain't wantin' no part of dis kind of trouble, Missus."

"You're at my mercy." She pivoted and locked the door.

Juniper moved away. "Please Missus, I can't be part of no such doings. Ain't fittin' nor proper."

"When he does whatever he wants, it doesn't make him a bad husband, so I can do whatever I want. You're legally subordinate to me." She smiled.

Sweat beaded on Juniper's brow, fear rising at the thought of a planter-class White woman's power to end his life. Catherine produced a bottle of whiskey and two shot glasses. She sipped from one and offered the other to Juniper.

He refused.

"I must admit that your dark skin intrigues me." Catherine took a longer draught of whiskey. She set the glass aside.

The spirits left her relaxed, confident, and energetic. Though she dared not openly admit her attraction, she lifted Juniper's shirt to touch his muscled abdomen. Unaware she labored under Aunt Sarah's spiritual assault, Catherine continued her twisted, irrational pursuit.

Juniper's voice quavered as Catherine's gaze lingered. "What you doin', Missus? Massa Brower ain't gonna stand for dis kind of thing. He de head of dis here house."

"Stop giving me petty excuses. Who said he has to know?"

"I's got to tend to dem field hands, den I gotta see dem horses get hitched proper." Juniper turned to leave.

Catherine forcefully pulled him to her. "If you walk out of this room, I'll scream. Then I'll tell everyone you raped me. Should I make a lesson out of you?"

"Lawd knows dis ain't right, Missus. You's one of dem fine Southern ladies of quality."

"Who, me?"

Catherine's breath caught as she touched his hands, feeling their roughness from labor. She gently traced his calluses. To Juniper, Catherine had transformed into a wicked, aggressive beast. He could not comprehend a White woman behaving this way. Having been the constant center of attention on plantations, Juniper had no desire to respond to sexual advances. Exhausted by being treated as an experiment, his manly pride lay wounded by masters who saw him only as breeding stock. His body served merely to generate profit. Though Catherine's energy differed, it disturbed him no less.

"I'll be the judge of that. I have the power. You don't have to play the victim. You are the victim. I picked you for a special job. It's time to show your gratitude for my generosity."

Catherine had granted Juniper a small garden plot to supplement the meager weekly rations of cornmeal and salt pork with greens.

"You can grow crops and keep the money from what you sell."

His elevation to overseer had brought countless privileges. At last, Catherine commanded a man.

"Juniper, you can be trusted to do things seen and unseen."

Having never loved Massa Brower unconditionally, she demonstrated this by placing Juniper's large hands upon her bosom, forcing him to grasp her flesh.

Juniper trembled, his voice failing. Catherine's brazen disrespect for her husband shocked and shamed him. "Missus!"

Words failed him as Catherine began unfastening her dress. She felt invigorated by the thrill of this forbidden encounter.

"I own you and everyone on this plantation. Don't you ever forget it."

She bound her favored slave to the bed and began tenderly massaging his large feet. Juniper found himself trapped during Catherine's daylong drinking binge. She poured spirits for them both. He timidly accepted the proffered glass while silently beseeching divine protection.

9

Freedom!

❖➤➤➤❮❮❮❖

The Texas sun bore down, scorching the earth beneath Aunt Sarah's weary feet, but the warmth no longer felt oppressive; instead, it cradled her spirit as she took a deep breath, her heart racing with elation. "I's free! I see de other side!"

Her body ached from the long journey; a series of trials carved into her bones. As she attempted to leap with joy, the sharp discomfort in her hips reminded her of her age and the hardships that had spanned decades, yet her soul soared. Aunt Sarah had evaded the heavy shackles of bondage, crossing state lines with the burden of fear nestled deep within her. Now, she marveled at the arid terrain of Mexico, which differed from the oppressive fields of the South.

Arriving at the Birthplace of the Blacks—El Nacimiento De los Negroes—she felt a sense of surreal disbelief. Here, the dry earth stretched out like an ancient quilt, sewn with the tales of those who had come before her. With a chuckle, she ripped off her horsehair wig, tossing it aside like the shackles of her past. Beneath the sun, her natural hair framed her face—a glorious white woolly mane that spoke of her resilience. It felt like a crown, a symbol of her hard-won victory.

Dust swirled around her as she stepped out of the covered wagon, the gritty coat of dirt clinging to her dress as a reminder of the obstacles she had endured. "I's thankin' de good Lawd above for carryin' me through dis journey to see a brighter day," she whispered, pressing her palms together in gratitude, her knuckles worn, yet strong from toil.

The trials of her escape surfaced in her mind, vivid and relentless. She recalled the treacherous swamps, where she crawled through thick, straggling weeds, her heart pounding as she lay flat on her belly, hidden from those who might seek to drag her back into chains. She had navigated through deep woods, crossed rivers where bears drank, and spent nights huddled in the dense foliage, fearful of the shadows that moved around her. Each close call had only fueled her resolve. She clenched her fists, determined: if she ever encountered a slave catcher, she'd fight tooth and nail.

Aunt Sarah paused, her breath heavy as she approached the banks of the Rio Grande. She felt the inviting pulse of freedom there—a pulse that thrummed in her chest like a drum. Mexico, with its history of abolishing slavery in 1837, offered a promise of life beyond the horrors she had known. This land was home to those like her—the Negroes Mascogos, descendants of resilient souls who had triumphed over suffering. They had carved out an existence in this fierce landscape, shaping a new life away from the cotton plantations of the Southern United States.

Sarah Ann, her steadfast ally, had crafted a daring plan to protect Aunt Sarah's journey. The Quakers, those altruistic souls who believed slavery was a sin, had turned their backs on the practice long ago, but even so, they had kept a distance. They gathered in hushed tones, their faces solemn as they plotted change, all while sitting across from the very people they worked to free.

During their secret meetings, Barbara had shared her thoughts, the lines of concern creasing her brow. "A free person who escapes to Canada or Mexico should not be returned to the owner." Shaking her head, Barbara's tone was grave. "In Canada, the harsh climate doesn't allow for crops that flourished on Southern plantations."

"I heard Aunt Sarah's son was sold in Texas. He's fled to Mexico." Sarah Ann's heart ached for the family torn apart.

"Getting her to Mexico won't be easy. It's a longer journey for a runaway." Barbara's eyes darted with worry.

"I must do this for her." Fierceness wreaked Sarah Ann's voice. "A mother and son must find their way back to each other."

Barbara nodded, but raised an eyebrow. "Mexico won't enforce a Fugitive Slave Act. If Aunt Sarah makes it there, she'll be free—but what will that mean for her?"

"She'll adapt for family. Isn't that worth the difference?" Sarah Ann stood on her conviction.

"You seem personally invested in this."

"I will not stay silent while my sister owns Aunt Sarah."

"Did I say something wrong?" Barbara tilted her head as she caught the flicker of pain in Sarah Ann's eyes.

"Forget it. We have work to do. There are stories of slaves from the South finding their place in Mexico—if their owners chase after them, there's a chance in court."

"The route through Texas is less organized, but I have contacts there."

"We can pull this off." Determination tightened Sarah Ann's jaw. "I'm ready to take risks for this cause."

For days, she had sheltered Aunt Sarah in secret, waiting for the right moment to send her off to freedom. Sarah Ann's heart ached at the thought of not accompanying the weary traveler until she got to the safe house, her throat thick with unshed tears.

As Aunt Sarah closed her eyes, visions of the past flooded her thoughts: the days of shucking corn, waking before dawn to stoke the fire, the rawness of her feet from endless labor. The dark memories pulled at her spirit as she lay beneath the stars, surrounded by the hushed songs of the night.

Time grew short. Advertisements would soon stain newspapers across Alabama, a weekly reminder that she was on the run—hunted and desired.

"Ain't all White folks got de devil in 'em. You's been de Lawd's own angel to me," Aunt Sarah mumbled in her sleep, her voice a lullaby of hope.

"God bless you, Aunt Sarah. You've given so much to others. Now, it's your turn to receive," Sarah Ann whispered, brushing an unruly curl from Aunt Sarah's forehead, her heart swelling with both fear and admiration.

As they prepared for the next leg of the journey, Sarah Ann bestowed Aunt Sarah with food and money, cementing the bond of trust between them. "Stay vigilant, Aunt Sarah. Don't look back, not for anything. We both have too much to lose."

"You done showed me de truth." Aunt Sarah's resolve had strengthened her weary body.

Each time fatigue threatened to take her down, she recalled Sarah Ann's words, clinging to the promise of liberation. Days melded into nights, but the goal of self-liberation illuminated her path.

However, as she approached the border of Mexico, doubt crept in like a shadow. Was the figure approaching her a slave catcher or a friend cloaked in the guise of danger? Trust was a gamble, but Aunt Sarah knew she had little choice—freedom was worth everything.

10

Power, Secrets, Scandals, and Lies

❦⟫⟫⟫ ⟪⟪⟪❦

It had been almost ten months since Aunt Sarah's mysterious departure from Rutherford Rocks.

Catherine had temporarily forgotten about Massa Brower's sins—having children with Hazel—when she finally pushed for the last time for a baby to leave her womb.

Massa Brower stood in the doorway of the dimly lit room. Enslaved women gathered around the bed, their hearts swelling with anticipation of cleaning up after Catherine's birthing experience. The White midwife coaxed Catherine to push harder, just one final time.

At that moment, Catherine found a reason to exert herself like never before. The pain of childbirth consumed her, forcing cries of agony from her lips. Sweat drenched her body, and fatigue weighed her down. She almost regretted becoming a mother.

"The baby's almost out! Push again!" the midwife encouraged urgently.

An enslaved woman released a blood-curdling scream upon noticing a shocking sight. The baby's head, crowned in coarse, tight curls, emerged from Catherine's body, dark as rich cocoa.

"Missus' baby's Black!" another woman screamed.

With alarm, they backed away from the bed as Massa Brower charged forward with heavy, deliberate steps.

Catherine felt her energy deplete as she faintly heard the word 'Black' echo in her ears, a cold realization settling in as she prepared to hold the infant to her breast.

The midwife covered her mouth with trembling hands. "Dear Jesus," she whispered.

The tension in the air grew thicker when Massa Brower snatched the curly-haired, mocha-colored infant boy from her arms.

"Don't kill 'em, Massa!" Tilly screamed, her voice brimming with terror.

Massa Brower appeared ready to choke the sweet baby around his neck with his bare hands. Tilly reached out to coax the newborn from his dangerous grip.

On that day, Juniper Junior was born, marking the beginning of the end of White supremacy in Alabama.

"What have you done?" Massa Brower yelled at Catherine, his fist clenched and brows furrowed in rage.

"Nothing. I've done nothing." Her voice was barely a whisper.

Catherine slowly pulled the white, sweat-drenched sheets over her face. Memories flooded her mind of one passionate night with Juniper that had turned into many when she'd done more than touch him out of curiosity. She'd forgotten about the time Juniper had been compelled to comply with all her wishes. While she knew her husband found solace in Hazel's arms—despite forcing his way inside of them—she had never intended to get pregnant by the slave with whom she had sought revenge on her husband. Ultimately, she did not suffer a miscarriage.

"You have nowhere to go," she had told Juniper when he tried to grab his shoes.

Catherine had pinned him down like an aggressor upon her prey. Juniper shook, fear coursing through him; he didn't even want to touch her.

"This time, I'll have my way." Catherine lay atop him.

Kiss by kiss, she envisioned taking revenge on her husband, giving Juniper a forbidden taste of sensuality. Catherine hadn't expected Juniper to awaken her senses in a way John Brower never had. She couldn't undo the sheet-pulling encounter that had ignited her body. She never thought she could get pregnant during her reckless escapades, but here she was, feeling alive, free, and in control as a woman through Juniper's touch. He had awakened a fierce lioness who kept returning to the den.

Massa Brower felt physically ill. He couldn't accept that Catherine had somehow slept with a Black man. The racist ripped the sheets from his wife's covered face. "Get it out of here! Get that Godforsaken Black bastard out of my sight before I kill his tiny ass!"

"You can't kill a baby—my baby," Catherine protested weakly.

"And you?" Massa Brower, with clenched teeth, shook his finger wildly in her face. "You lying about a whole lot."

The enslaved women concealed the baby, fearing for his little life.

Massa Brower towered over Catherine. "Who is it?"

"Who what?"

"Who's the father?"

The thought of public shame and the complications of his wife's indiscretion caused him to drop to his knees, weighed down by his troubled soul.

"You," she lied with desperation.

"You slept with a slave. Had to. No one near Rutherford Rocks is free." John's voice was tinged with venom.

"That's preposterous," Catherine said, weakly laughing, her mind racing.

"Is it now?"

Her head bobbed from fatigue.

"Missus tired and weak after having the baby. Please, let 'er rest," the midwife pleaded.

Massa stood up and rubbed his temples, frustration bubbling to the surface. He was adept at dishing out oppression and infidelity but struggled to bear the lashings returned to him. Catherine had given her husband the painful revenge she desired. Since Catherine was a White woman, the heir of Rutherford Rocks would be free and entitled to inherit every inch of the plantation. He pushed the sheet from his wife's face, his rage uncontainable.

"Don't tell me how to talk to *my* wife! There's a problem here, and I'm gon' get to the bottom of it!" Massa Brower hollered. "Don't make me ask you again. Who's the father?" He shook Catherine's shoulders.

"I already told you. It's your baby. Calm down. You're hurting me."

Massa Brower began dragging her out of bed. "I want the name of the traitor who got in my bed!"

His desire to end the relationship with Catherine burned hot. "I want a divorce! I'll never love you again!"

Catherine didn't feel her husband had ever truly loved her. She didn't need him for money; life at Rutherford Rocks had hardened her sensibilities. She wanted to laugh openly in John's face, confessing her illicit deeds, but she held her tongue as her body slid across the floor.

The midwife pushed John Brower forcefully. "Leave her be!"

He whipped around to face the midwife. "Do you expect me to be nice about this? Maybe I should just kill *her* now instead!"

With a sudden burst of rage, his hand came down like an ax across Catherine's face, causing tears to stream down her cheeks.

The midwife grabbed a whip from across the room that was normally used to threaten enslaved workers. "Leave her be, I said!"

As he started to choke his wife, the midwife lashed John Brower across the back with all her might.

Catherine gasped, growing faint.

When John winced in pain, the midwife swiftly restrained him with the whip, wrapping it around his neck. He coughed uncontrollably, desperation in his eyes, as he stammered, gasping for breath.

He fell and struck his head on a chamber pot. John briefly gasped shallowly, crawling on all fours a short distance as blood poured from his nose. Everyone watched in disbelief, failing to summon immediate help. The struggle had caused a massive heart attack. A thud reverberated through the room. John fought for breath, struggling to keep his eyes open, but they shut one last time. A final time. Rutherford Rocks would never be the same again. John Brower was dead.

11

Home Sweet Home

❖⟫⟫⟩⟨⟨⟨❖

Aunt Sarah noticed that the figure at the Texas-Mexico border didn't resemble a White man but rather looked like a Black Indian. Taking a leap of faith, she chose to follow him, trusting her instincts that it was safe.

"No hablo Inglés." The man gestured apologetically, indicating he did not speak English.

The Spanish-speaking Black Seminole guided her to a gathering place, bustling with locals.

"Nacimiento," he said, nodding with pride.

Aunt Sarah's heart swelled with disbelief; she had never imagined that colored people were in Mexico. They stopped in front of a quaint single-story structure with a tiled roof, its vibrant colors beckoning her closer. Clutching her walking stick and a small bag, and although she couldn't read, she found herself entranced by a hand-painted sign that announced, in jubilant hues, the promise of life ahead.

As she stepped out, Aunt Sarah felt a wave of confusion wash over her, mingled with the discomfort of sweat clinging to her clothes. A man stood on the steps of the store, a warm smile breaking across his face as he waved enthusiastically. He sprinted toward her, the joy radiating from him shining through.

At first, Aunt Sarah was unsure of the reason for her presence, but when the man came face-to-face with her, her lip quivered in disbelief. In that moment, the fire of a mother's love ignited within her as she realized she was finally looking into the eyes of her firstborn child.

"Warren!" she screamed, tears spilling down her cheeks, realizing she had found her child at last.

Warren mirrored Aunt Sarah's features—his face, his eyes, and his rich, mahogany complexion spoke volumes of their shared lineage. He enveloped her in a tight embrace, and they held each other, overwhelmed by the magnitude of their reunion.

With tears welling in his eyes and choked by emotions, he could hardly speak. "I didn't think I'd ever see you again." He pressed his lips to her cheek. "I felt so lonely without you. I never forgot my momma."

"I'm sorry I wasn't there for you." Aunt Sarah's heart was heavy with regret.

Instead of crumbling under the weight of abandonment, Warren had emerged as a strong-willed perfectionist, deeply aware that no one would come to save him. He had mastered Spanish and was adept in English, embodying resilience forged by necessity. Warren understood that nothing could replace the warmth of parental love.

"There's someone else who wants to meet you. Come inside." Warren gently tugged on her hand.

Aunt Sarah felt a rush of self-consciousness as she followed, her apprehension bubbling to the surface. "I's filthy with dirt and sweat." She glanced down at her worn clothes.

"You don't have to defend your appearance. You're here, and that's what matters most."

"I 'preciate all dis, but I feels ashamed. After all dese years, I don' want my son ta see me like dis."

Her head hung low, but despite the shame, Warren smiled. "Will you be okay? I'll be right back."

She nodded, and Warren made a silent pact with her that allowed her to keep her dignity intact. He returned moments later, a stunning long cultural dress draped over his arm. It was a garment reminiscent of those Hazel and her daughter, Rosalind, might wear. A sense of anger within Aunt Sarah was calmed by Warren's words.

"This is for you."

Aunt Sarah's eyes widened with astonishment. "Whar you git all dat money from? You ain't been stealin', is ya?"

"I worked for it. I own this store. I can take you to a place to get cleaned up first." There was pride in his voice.

"Did ya say own?" Aunt Sarah followed Warren around the corner, her heart racing.

He opened the door and handed her lye soap, a soft cloth, and a tub of water.

"That's what I said. This is my house. I'll be back after I give you time to freshen up." Warren kissed her gently on the cheek.

Standing in awe, Aunt Sarah couldn't believe she had access to fresh water without having to trek to a creek or wait for rain. She scrubbed her skin until it glowed, cleaner than it had been in her entire life. A sweet, inviting scent hung in the air as she opened the door, her heart soaring at the sight of a new pair of leather shoes that made her want to leap like a carefree child. Sarah Ann's hope for Aunt Sarah's better life was finally coming true.

"I got me a new life now!" Aunt Sarah exclaimed joyfully.

She was startled when she noticed a woman across the room, a comb carved from bone in one hand and a container of herbal paste in the other. The stranger slipped out the door, leaving behind the intoxicating fragrance. Aunt Sarah inhaled deeply before rubbing the paste onto her silver strands, feeling regal and renewed.

"How it be possible I look dis nice?" She gazed at her reflection in the long mirror, tears streaming down her face at the sight before her. Years of being deprived of self-worth and beauty melted away in an instant.

Aunt Sarah felt liberated from the struggles that had weighed so heavily on her shoulders for so long. In this vibrant new place, the limitations imposed upon her began to dissolve, allowing her to embrace the richness of her identity.

A gentle tap on the door jolted her from her thoughts. Warren entered, a bright smile lighting up his face.

"You're *so* beautiful. I love it on you." His eyes shone with admiration. "Now, will you come with me?"

"Yessuh!" Aunt Sarah followed her son around the corner, excitement bubbling within her.

"Try walking in it. If it's too long, I can hem it for you, Momma."

"I's happy now! Dis the best dress I eva had. Thank you. Ya know how to sew?"

"I wash dishes, cook, sew, clean, and do a whole lot more. I have to. Men like me don't have limits. We soar." Warren opened the front door for her.

Sunlight poured through the windowpane, illuminating Aunt Sarah's smooth skin and her spirit.

"I'd like you to meet my wife, Lucy." Warren gestured toward a woman nearby. "She speaks a little English but mostly Spanish."

Aunt Sarah blinked in awe, taking in the beauty of the moment.

"And this here is my little one, Joe. Josefina."

The sight of the baby brought tears to Aunt Sarah's eyes.

She envisioned teaching her granddaughter the games she had played with White children, hoping to invest in her own flesh and blood.

Warren hoisted Josefina into the air, a wide grin stretching across his face as Aunt Sarah's heart filled with joy.

"She sho' is pretty as a mornin' glory. Let me hold my grandbaby chile?"

"She's coming your way." Warren placed the baby into his mother's arms.

"You sho' is a plump and hearty little miss. Look at dem rosy cheeks, sweet as sugar!" Aunt Sarah cooed, her heart swelling with love. "Do you see how de good Lawd done blessed you wit' such beauty?"

Lucy chuckled as she placed a cup of cool water on a wooden table across the room. She enriched the setting with sofkee—a corn-based soup cooked with ash—and a beef tamale, alongside utensils for dining. Lucy approached Aunt Sarah, beckoning her gently.

"Venga," she said. "Come."

Though Lucy had never experienced enslavement, her sensitivity to Aunt Sarah's plight was palpable. After blessing her meal, Aunt Sarah's gaze lingered over the food. There were no remnants of cornbread baked in ashes, no fatback or vegetables, nor fish caught from streams or trapped animals. Aunt Sarah was accustomed to eating with her fingers, scraping together what little meat she could find. Hazel and her children feasted upon finer foods, while the best ingredients had never graced Aunt Sarah's lips.

Lucy arranged Aunt Sarah's meal atop a plate, providing her with silverware for her use.

Warren noticed her hesitation. "What's wrong?"

"I neva' seen food like dis befo'."

Warren smiled. "Your diet will change. We eat differently."

"Yessuh. It do look good." Aunt Sarah attempted to mask her unease.

As she reached for her food, her hesitance bubbled back to the surface, and she jumped up.

"Where are you going, Momma?"

"To a cabin, to eat with the other niggers. Where should I go?"

"We don't use anti-Negro slurs, stereotypes, or colorist comments here. This community is meant to empower us all. You can eat at the table," Warren said firmly.

"I 'members well when dey near beat de life outta dat po' soul for some missin' corn. Tell me true now - dis here food belong to you proper? Don't want no mo' whuppins on nobody's back." Aunt Sarah's mind raced with memories of pain.

"I pay for everything that I have. Like I told you before, nothing is stolen. You can have what you want to eat, Momma. Would you please enjoy your food now?" Warren urged gently.

"I's sorry." Aunt Sarah sensed she'd upset him. "I's been eatin' wit my hands all my days. Ain't never had no fine silverware nor seen my food on one dem china plates."

Warren's heart ached with both fury and tenderness as he watched his mother shrink from the simple dignities of freedom. Years of bondage had taught her to see herself as less than human, to question even her right to use a fork or plate. The way she marveled at his achievements while doubting her own worth kindled a deep rage in him against those who had broken her spirit yet filled him with gentle patience for the woman who had endured so much.

"They tried to kill the human being in you, Momma," he whispered, his voice thick with emotion, "but they couldn't do it. You survived. You made it here to freedom, and I'm going to help you remember who you really are."

He knew the journey ahead would be long—not just the healing of her body from years of toil, but the awakening of her soul to its own dignity. Every time she flinched from sitting at a proper table or hesitated to speak her mind, he felt the weight of generations of oppression. Yet in her very presence here in Mexico, in her courage to flee, he saw the unquenchable spirit they had failed to destroy.

Prosperity was a radical concept Warren had learned to embrace in Mexico, even before he met William Ellis, "Guillermo Enrique Eliseo," a formerly enslaved African-American who became a Mexican millionaire. If anyone tried to bother a formerly enslaved person in Mexico, he knew they would have to fight for their right to exist.

Warren approached his mother, bending down and wrapping her in a warm embrace. Without speaking, Warren picked up the silverware, placing it in her hands while swallowing back tears.

"Use the silverware today. Use it every day unless you're eating food that can only be eaten with your fingers. Please. You deserve more than the crumbs of life. No matter your color or race, we all do."

"It skeers my mind to see our colored folks in charge of anythin'. All I ever knowed was cookin' and servin' de White folks - ain't nobody never treated me like I's worth puttin' food on a plate for. Lawd knows, in all my days, ain't nobody even handed me a plain bowl of mush wit' they own hands. Dey's so much to learn, and my po' head can't hardly stand it." A knot tightened in her throat.

Warren patted her hand. "Nothing has to hold you back now if you don't want it to. Your queenly crown has been restored. We don't see ourselves as victims here, and taking care of family is my priority."

Aunt Sarah ate her unfamiliar food with a mixture of gratitude and nervousness. It didn't taste like anything she was used to, but it was far from bad. She tasted beans and tortillas, feeling hesitant but willing to embrace new experiences. The thought of learning Spanish frightened her, and she felt a pang of shame at her inability to read or write in English.

A customer entered Warren's store, and Aunt Sarah's heart leaped with joy upon discovering that her son owned a dry goods business. Rows of corn, beans, rice, bread, household goods, clothing, and medical herbs adorned the neatly kept establishment. Warren refused to be overworked, underpaid, or fall into debt—determined to provide a comfortable life for those he loved. He recalled the years he spent without shoes until he was thirteen, the loose shirt hanging on his small frame as he was torn from his mother's side. More than anything, he was resolved to create a different future for himself and the next generation—one where he would never again bear the burden of a hoe on his shoulder as he trudged into the sweltering fields.

As Aunt Sarah observed her son scribbling in a ledger while customers took goods on credit, she marveled at his newfound confidence.

"I'll be back on payday," one customer assured as he departed.

"Look how my boy done turned out—handsome as de mornin' sun and sharp as a whip. De Lawd's mercy done been pourin' down on my chile all dese years." Aunt Sarah beamed. "I's proud dat you talk so good."

Warren had come a long way since his days as a water boy in the fields, maturing into a man who placed immense value on family and financial stability. He believed that strategic rebellion through education and knowledge was a powerful means of enacting change. As a shop owner, he had become influential in the community while building a better life— something Aunt Sarah wished she could have done.

"Running a store suits me. I don't owe nobody, but people owe me. I do not accept my position to barely survive. Negroes do not have to behave as victims."

"I's mighty proud. Yous seem ta have plenty of everything."

"Except for a momma." Warren's tone softened as he attempted to help her understand. "That's gonna change."

"If I could teach myself to speak and read a new language, so can you, Momma."

Aunt Sarah stood as she cleaned up her dishes, anxiety creeping in at the thought of leaving anything dirty behind. She felt that what was done could not be undone. Decades of conditioning had robbed her of the ability to see herself as deserving.

Lucy stopped her.

"She'll do it, Momma."

"She will?"

Lucy smiled brightly. "Sí!"

"What 'bout choppin' wood, cookin', milkin' cows? I gots ta do sumthin' ta keep muhself goin'."

Warren felt a mix of frustration and compassion at his mother's overly submissive demeanor.

"You don't need to do that anymore. You're free here. And if anyone comes trying to bother you, the community will help me take care of it. Slave catchers aren't welcomed here, legally or socially."

Aunt Sarah felt a wave of fear wash over her, her body turning heavy with doubt. She wanted to believe her son, but the ghosts of her past held her in chains of disbelief.

Warren stepped closer, fully understanding that the world rarely sympathized with the emotional scars left by enslavement. It was his mission to help mend the fractures in his mother's spirit.

"It's time to change the way you think. You're no longer a slave."

"I don't know how ta be anybody else. What am I den?"

"A mother, grandmother, and human being. Take a little time off. I want you to feel safe and comfortable. Just be happy." Warren smiled.

He noticed Aunt Sarah's gaze fixate on a bookshelf, curiosity brewing in the depths of her eyes.

"Do you know how to read?"

"Not a word."

"All those years ago, when I was a little boy sold for trying to learn to read didn't go to waste. I want to teach you, Momma. I've been to a real school." Warren pulled a book from the middle of the shelf. "This here is my favorite."

As Aunt Sarah sat quietly, taking in the words as her son read a story she'd never heard, tears streamed down her cheeks. "That was beautiful."

Warren turned the page, moving closer to her, pointing at a single letter. "This is called 'A.' Say 'A' for me, Momma."

"A."

As Warren continued to guide her through the letters of the alphabet, Aunt Sarah discovered a newfound confidence swelling within her. Each "A" and "B" she spoke grew louder, more assertive, until they reached "Z." When the lesson concluded, Warren gently patted her hand.

"You will learn to read. I'll teach you myself."

With her head held high, Aunt Sarah followed Warren to another place, stepping into a brightly painted structure adorned with a long porch.

"Dis feel like home," Aunt Sarah declared, a sense of belonging washing over her.

"Because that's what it is."

As Aunt Sarah basked in the joy of reuniting with Warren and his family, a shadow of unfinished business loomed over her heart. Her other children still lingered in Rutherford Rocks, and while she was grateful for her new life, the ache of separation pierced her. The bond between a mother and her children was sacred—an eternal connection not defined only by their infancy but also as they ventured toward adulthood. However, this depth of awareness was a luxury often denied to enslaved people, yet it laid the foundation for future leaders rising amidst oppression.

Aunt Sarah marveled at her son's growth since the last time she had been present in his life. She thought of Sarah Ann's gift of closure, a gentle push toward raising her self-esteem. Few enslaved mothers had the chance to reunite with their children, but Aunt Sarah delighted in the rare blessing that had been bestowed upon her.

"I's luv ya, Warren." Her voice trembling with sincerity.

Warren bent down, kissing her cheek once more. "I waited most of my life to hear those words from you again." Tears glistened in his eyes.

Aunt Sarah felt the weight of her other children pulling at her heartstrings. The need to be there for them stabbed at her soul, permeating the tired bones of her long journey, even though they were far away from the hay mattress where she once slept.

12

Duped

❖⟫⟫⟫⟪⟪⟪❖

Word spread about Aunt Sarah's successful liberation. Her body was not found; she was assumed to be alive, somewhere, somehow. Aunt Sarah became a plantation hero to the enslaved masses of people who wished they could disappear without consequences.

The time hadn't come to tell her story, so the world didn't hear about how she'd arrived in Mexico and who helped her, but bigger problems unfolded at Rutherford Rocks.

Catherine's affair with Juniper had spread through the plantation like wildfire, and the evidence had come to light. Juniper came to Catherine's bedside, wanting to lay eyes on the controversial newborn he'd heard about. It never crossed his mind that the baby hadn't been Massa's. Impregnating a White woman was far-fetched and unfathomable. He thought enslaved workers had made up the cruel rumor to scare him.

Juniper had seen Catherine take herbal concoctions; she said it was to prevent pregnancy. He was feeling drowned in confusing thoughts.

"Lemme see dat baby," Juniper demanded.

Catherine wailed over her husband's lifeless body. The White midwife couldn't get a pulse. A gash in his head was bloody, raw, messy, and putrid. Juniper carefully stepped backward, unaware that Massa Brower was dead. He was shocked. He warned Catherine that being aggressive with him would turn into a problem.

The midwife ran out of the room past Juniper. The doctor and authorities arrived, declaring John Brower dead. Catherine lied on Juniper, framing him for everything. She refused to look bad; there was no way she would be taken off her Southern Belle pedestal or dilute her greatness.

"I'm scared to death of Juniper. He raped me and killed my husband because John tried to stand up to him about the assault. Juniper did it all. He fought John, pushed him, and now my husband is dead," Catherine tearfully told the sheriff.

Juniper listened. He grew more uncomfortable while thinking of everything Catherine forced him to do.

"Naw suh, dat ain't what happened at all. I jes' got here myself. Don't know nuthin' 'bout what Missus sayin'. Was a woman done run outta here 'fore either one of y'all showed up," he explained, his heart nearly skipping beats.

Dogs and gun-wielding men circled the plantation. They didn't have to hunt Juniper down; the big, burly Negro overseer was theirs to take. A White woman had given her account of events, so it had to be true. Not one enslaved person would defend Juniper. Fear engulfed him.

"Won't nobody open dey mouth and tell de truth 'bout what went on?" He looked around.

They recalled the way he'd treated them, especially Rufus. Juniper's eyes caught Rufus' gaze. It was Rufus' turn to make Juniper look like a brutal buffoon. Rufus had been trained to work harder. He had come to take Catherine's bloody towels to dispose of them so Juniper wouldn't beat him. He stood sure-footed while cleaning up from childbirth alongside his wife, who assisted the midwife.

Rufus looked away, unable to part his lips. Juniper was supposed to be his racial brother, but he'd betrayed him because of his power. And now, Juniper needed him and his wife to plant doubt in the sheriff's mind. Rufus' manhood had been unjustly broken. His hernia prevented him from working as fast as Juniper wanted in the field. The wound of betrayal cut deep. Juniper let them live in slave cabins that were too hot or too cold. He fit the profile of a terrible killer if Mistress Catherine said so. The enslaved workers chatted about how often Catherine forced the man who had been heartless to them to comply with her sexual demands. His pleas and screams were memorable. He didn't want his life to end for touching her.

"Is dey anybody here got de nerve to speak up 'gainst what dis woman sayin'? Please, somebody tell 'em I ain't done nuthin' wrong! She ain't no victim—I's de one sufferin' here! She been keepin' quiet 'bout who she been layin' wit!"

Juniper's plea fell on deaf ears. The room was quiet and still. Not even dust moved through the tense air. He had done Catherine's bidding with extra doses of cruelty, so Juniper had no allies. Although he had been manipulated and raped, it was his turn to be judged harshly. And so he was. The story that stuck was that the overseer murdered the master, sexually assaulted his wife, and produced a baby. Looking at Juniper's size, no one would believe that Catherine had overpowered him. No one even cared.

Juniper was big and strong, and was used as a breeder on three other plantations. He fathered ten children at Banks Plantation, eight at Sands Gates Plantation, and twelve at Sunnyside Plantation. Two of the children at Sunnyside died after owners sold Juniper, yet again. Forced to move from cabin to cabin each time he impregnated an enslaved women who were also big and strong, there was an expectation of them to produce hard-working offspring with superhuman powers. He never had a family of his own in a loving way. This is how he became disconnected from humanity when encountering other enslaved workers. Now, people hated him for a personality that wasn't his fault. His mistresses used his body to produce another child. His heart was broken beyond repair, but she lied about how an innocent life that he would've wanted to protect and love came to be.

"My loving husband is gone. He meant the world to me." Catherine tried to convince the sheriff of Juniper's motive. She sniffed. "And now there's a nigger baby that came out of me. I'll never recover. Take him—please. Make him pay for this. My life is ruined!"

"Shame on you, Missus, for tellin' such stories 'gainst me!" Juniper hollered.

The sheriff's eyes narrowed. He thought about Juniper's disregard for laws and accountability. He dared to violate a White woman. He dared to kill a man who enslaved him. The conspiracy was treated as fact. His poor investigation was over. The real power lay in the power of hate and fear.

"That's enough, nigger. You're coming with us."

Eight more men barreled through the door, eager to restrain Juniper. He disappeared while kicking and screaming. "De truth don't mean nothin' to none of y'all! Missus de evil one here, tellin' lies to destroy a po' slave! She de one what come after me—bound me up like a hog for slaughter. I's cried and pleaded wit' her to leave me in peace, fo' de Lawd I did!"

"Nobody wants to bed a nigger. You heathens can't wait to get your hands on a White woman. I never heard anything as ridiculous as this," the sheriff said.

Catherine's effort paid off, although she didn't have to work hard to frame a man who she'd sexually assaulted. She breathed easier when she realized she had successfully dehumanized Juniper as if he weren't a real person. She had done what was best for her mentally.

"Take the murderer and rapist away before he hurts someone else!" Catherine said, thinking, *Thank God there will be no more conversation about this.*

No one cared that Juniper was about to die because of a lie, not even the woman who crafted the evil tale.

The tragic news spread to all the slave quarters. Slaves emerged from the darkness, appearing with trembling steps, deeply concerned, looking anxiously at one another.

"Massa, I's knowed you all my born days! Not you, Massa, please!" one woman cried as if she had been blessed to have him in her life. She was one of the slaves Catherine had brought to Rutherford Rocks.

Catherine turned her head to take a closer look at who lamented over her husband. She wondered why she was so attached to John, a man who had too many plantation relationships that made her stomach turn.

"Water. I need water," she said.

The midwife brought her a sip of water to calm her grief. She had a bigger problem than her husband's death.

13

The House of Pain

Two men were dead: one enslaved and one free.

"Massa done left dis earth. I knows you grievin' for him. Dat Juniper done killed de one who kept food in all our mouths. What's gonna become of us po' colored folks now?" Rhodie stood next to Mistress Chatherine's bed. "You ain't left dis bed since we buried Massa in de cold ground. You wastin' away to nuthin' cause you won't touch no food. Dem po' horses ain't got enough in dey bellies. Reckon since you ain't usin' dis food, maybe dem horses should?"

Catherine rested as Rhodie tried to help her regain her energy. She lay listless and despondent in bed.

"Sometimes you talk too much, Rhodie. Shut up!"

"Do askin' iffin ya want more tea in ya glass over der count, Missus?"

"No tea. Whiskey. Straight. Every time."

"Is you sho' bout dat? Seems like you and dat whiskey been mighty close friends dese days."

Catherine stumbled out of bed, looking around for her whip. She weakly swung it at Rhodie, although she was barely able to stand. "Just do what I tell you. You're too saucy! You don't know what it's like to be a widow. You're just a slave. I still have rights to all of you at Rutherford Rocks!"

"Dat's true, Missus. I's jest tryin' to find out what ta do for ya."

When Aunt Sarah left, Rhodie had to work like her little legs never got tired. She watched the other cooks make Catherine's food, and Rhodie carried out her mistress's personal errands.

"Out of everyone here, I trust you more than anyone now that Aunt Sarah is gone."

Catherine had drained all the whiskey to escape her problems. Rhodie had no more to pour for her when the last five drops dripped into the glass.

"Das it!"

Catherine angrily glared at the glass. "Find more."

"Das all dere wuz, Missus."

"Go make some then."

"I 'on't know how." Rhodie shrugged.

"I need a drink. Find me something!" Catherine banged her fists on her legs.

Rhodie happily left her room to try to scrounge around for liquor. She headed to the slave quarters, hoping someone could share whatever they had.

Catherine's head fell back onto the pillow. Her right arm flopped on the side of the bed. She felt weary from struggling to maintain authority. Juniper wasn't around to keep the enslaved workers in line. Massa Brower's lack of presence brought a new set of problems. Plantation life had been disrupted. Rutherford Rocks was facing foreclosure, but Catherine was keeping that dirty secret to herself.

The plantation cost a lot to run, despite workers not needing to be paid because they provided free labor. Catherine was now responsible for keeping all financial records, paying bank notes, and maintaining the plantation account books. Before, her primary duty had been attending slave auctions and recording the purchases of slaves. She began fumbling around with papers after her drinking tirades. There was nearly nothing left in the bank.

"They're all shady crooks," she complained, reading each bill.

Catherine owed a lot of people money, not because she hadn't been financially responsible, but because of things her husband had done in the dark. She had no idea John Brower had been gambling profits when he was away from the plantation. John's creditors were unaware of how much property belonged to his wife, how much they jointly owned, and how little only belonged to him. His misrepresentation of his financial standing allowed him to gain favor. Interest piled up on unpaid debts. Catherine worried that she'd have to sort out property ownership issues in court. Rutherford Rocks was also in great need of maintenance, but Catherine didn't want to spend any money on making substantial repairs until debts had been properly addressed. She began to feel overwhelmed.

"What did John do?" Crying, she balled her fist in frustration.

The enslaved workers hadn't run away because they had nowhere to go or didn't want to leave family and friends behind. Tater still rang a bell at four in the morning to get the day's work started in the fields. Since there was no overseer, he took it upon himself to help his missus out until further notice. Enslaved workers continued to faithfully harvest crops and take good care of them. Field hands had been trained to work hard and care about their work. Additionally, Catherine's baby, Isaiah, wouldn't stop screaming or eating. She knew she'd need more help around the house with Aunt Sarah, Juniper, and John Brower gone. Catherine felt overwhelmed, needing to run a plantation and raise a Negro baby who shared her blood.

Rita, a fifteen-year-old who had just had a baby on the plantation, fed the little boy and took care of him as her own. John Brower had added her to the rotation of enslaved women in his feather bed. Lucy, another enslaved woman, told Rita to chew cotton root and keep it hidden under her bed to prevent pregnancy.

"Massa can put de lash to my back if I ain't quick enough wit' his wants. I ain't givin' him nothin' to whup me for," Rita told Lucy.

"Ain't no freedom for dem slave chilluns. De mama in chains, de babies in chains too. When Massa plant his seed in you, dat baby his property same as you is. All dat sufferin' you takes from Massa ain't no love thing - dat's pure evil he doin' to yo' body. You ain't no different from de rest of us. He fillin' his pockets off our broken backs and dese precious babies too."

Rita ignored those facts. She thought about the dirt floor in the slave quarters. She grew tired of having the worst food that was barely suitable for an animal to eat. When Rita questioned him about dealing with his wife or Hazel, he privately told her that he didn't care.

"Were you expecting to hear that I love my wife or a slave? The more slaves that are born, the more profit I get from their labor. Come here, gal," Massa Brower had said, laughing.

Rita ignored Lucy's advice and eagerly complied with his wishes because she noticed all the privileges Hazel had. However, Brower had died before she could reap her rewards.

She was left to be a wet nurse to his wife's Negro baby while caring for her own.

Catherine tried to become more hands-on with her son. "What's happening to me? I barely have time to take a nap."

She called on Rita to give her a break by looking after her son, whom she called Isaiah. Rita's body was being forced to its limits. She had nothing to show for it like she thought she would. She returned to the Negro cabins, known as the slave quarters, and didn't get a spot in the Great House like Hazel. The only perk was that she didn't have to work in the fields.

Lucy looked at her. "Wipe your tears. You didn't listen to me. Now ya gotsta work this thing out."

∽∾

Rutherford Rocks had once been busy with endless lunches and dinner parties. Catherine finally had one visitor check on her after John Brower died, and the plantation had become eerily quiet. Mrs. Mary Rector's husband was a member of the Alabama legislature. Her husband, Tom Rector, was a United States senator. Like Catherine, the master's wife had grown up in a slaveholding family that had been touched by capitalism and bigotry. She was given slaves as gifts from her father. Senator Rector had ten before he met her. They had plenty of balls and dinner meetings.

Mary smiled and often appeared reserved, but hearing gossip about Catherine touched her sensibilities. She understood what it was like to live in a house of pain—one that was big and fancy on the inside—where unhappiness ruled.

"I'm sorry for the loss of your husband."

"Thank you, Mrs. Rector."

Catherine was recovering from a hangover. She didn't feel like entertaining company, but she didn't want to be rude.

"It's Mary, and there's another reason I stopped by."

"Which is?"

"I'd rather be blunt than join in gossip with the other ladies. Get ahold of yourself, Catherine. We all know that the little Negro you gave birth to was the overseer's child. Place it with another slave and say it's hers. A White woman can't keep this sort of child. Your drinking is destroying Rutherford Rocks. You better turn things around fast."

"A lot of you need to worry about your own marriages and relationships. I am over needing to be liked by you or the rest of the hypocrites who were my so-called slaveholding friends."

"I haven't known you as long as some of the other wives who also attended dinners at Rutherford Rocks, but I'm trying to help you. That's why I'm here. I'm concerned about your reputation and welfare."

"Why do you care so much?" Catherine struggled to hold her eyes open.

"Listen, I know what you did to Juniper and why. I made the same mistake with a slave. You're not the first or last who will play with them, but what you can't do is get pregnant and tell the world."

Catherine's mouth dropped. Deep inside, she was still a heartless woman. She didn't feel a twinge of guilt that Juniper had been hung. When Catherine was a little girl, she'd seen several slaves killed in front of her. Catherine was surprised that other women in her social circle had been intimate with their slaves.

"Some people will wonder how you really felt about John Brower. They won't want to do business with a woman who willingly had relations with a male slave. Women can't do what men can. Tighten up your ship or it's going to sink fast. Don't overplay your hand."

Catherine looked at Mary with tears in her eyes. "I want to keep my baby. He came from me. He's mine, and I'm grateful that God gave me a child of any color. I didn't mean for any of this to happen, but how can I hate my own flesh?"

Mary sighed. "Slavery is complicated and hard. There are lots of things about it no one meant to happen. It causes strain on the good and bad people who really don't want to be brutal. It's just required."

"I didn't ask to be born a mistress."

"And the women we own didn't ask to be born slaves."

"I had my choice of suitors, and I got stuck with John Brower. Both of us running Rutherford Rocks was a lot of pressure. Now, he's gone." Catherine rubbed her temples.

"He died first. Count your blessings that John Brower won't be able to insult you anymore. Marriage is a contract. Enjoy the financial security and power that it offers."

The two women hugged. Slavery was rough on the bodies of people who were owned, but people who benefited from owning them did not escape the consequences of profitability. It was an undiscussed truth that removed favor, peace, and happiness from their bloodlines.

"I don't know what to do. I'm in over my head."

"I'm here to help, not judge. May I?"

"Three hundred years from now, would you want the truth of our stories to be told?"

"No. I wouldn't want people to know how bad it was for them or us. I hope stories like this never leave one set of lips."

They shared a tender moment that was frozen in time. Newfound camaraderie was cathartic. The women sat up until the wee hours of the morning venting to each other about the pressures of being influential plantation wives.

"My husband made babies with four of our slave women. I know how much it hurts. As a political wife, I have to keep my mouth shut and my head turned. All of this is between you and me, I hope."

"Of course it is. How can they want both slaves and wives?"

"I've never met a man who doesn't want it all."

"I suppose you're right. John was parading around with a slave that I inherited and brought here. Don't they see what it does to us? Slaves dug his grave, and then I watched Hazel and my husband's children weep over the freshly turned dirt. I never had a chance to know what it felt like to be the mother of his child."

"Lies are common on plantations. Everyone is wrapped up in them. The money from slavery and the mindsets of men come from the devil, not God. Don't pity these ignorant slaveholding men. When they die unexpectedly, their death brings both relief and sorrow. They started this, but don't let it ruin your life. Let John Brower rest in hell. My own husband's time shall come someday. Until then, I will smile in public although he let me down as a man." Mary added, "But my visit is about you and only you, Catherine."

Catherine nodded slowly.

"At least you won't have to look over your shoulder anymore, wondering what John is doing and with whom."

"He ruined my life. I was tired of being used and abused."

Mary picked up a brush to neaten her friend's hair. "It's been a long time since I've had a talk like this. Many of us have stood where you stand now. This too shall pass."

"Thanks for coming. I apologize for snapping at you. I'm not feeling well.

"You're drunk."

"Not anymore."

"You know what I mean."

"Maybe you are a true friend. What do I do now?"

Catherine jumped when she heard a tap at her door. Her friend placed the brush on a nightstand.

"He ate real good, Missus," Rhodie said, handing the baby to Catherine.

Catherine thanked her and closed the door.

"What's his name?" Mary moved closer to take a good look at the baby.

"I called him Juniper Junior at first. Now, I say he's Isaiah."

"I like Isaiah better. He looks like an Isaiah. I bet he'll grow up to be strong and smart. Let me hold Isaiah if you don't mind. I don't want to hurt him."

Catherine gently handed him to Mary. "His eyes and skin remind me of one of the little slave boys who grew up to do carpenter work. He had a little toy by my bed when he was young. His mother died from a high fever. He was a sweet boy."

Mary was already fond of Isaiah. He had a sweet disposition and a mesmerizing smile.

"I could stay up all night holding you. You're such an adorable baby boy. I know the loving embrace of a mother. Your mammy is really Catherine, isn't she, boy? And she doesn't feel you're really Negro inside because you came from her," Mary told Isaiah.

"What did you just say?"

"You heard me," Mary responded sharply. "This baby is yours. I know."

The same women who despised enslaved people because of their color and race found a way to also love them at times. Isaiah was one such example. Mary sat down in a wooden rocking chair.

"He's fast asleep now." Mary handed him back to Catherine.

Catherine held her son while hoping he would be entitled to every inch of land when she died. She didn't tell Mary that she wanted Isaiah to be the sole heir of Rutherford Rocks to disgrace her husband's painful legacy. Mary was a seasoned political wife who could anticipate some of the things Catherine was thinking.

"I know that you're confused. Don't let too much humanity creep into your heart. It's time to make plans and implement them. This situation is too scandalous. Isaiah must be sold before anyone figures out what really happened. Send him to another plantation. If you don't, someone will probably kill him. A mob will burn this plantation down to the ground if more people hear about a scandal like this."

"I've already had too much blood on my hands and hate in my heart."

Mary shook her head. "You're a White woman who claimed a slave sexually assaulted you. I warned you how bad things can get. Control the story. Don't let it control you."

Tears filled Catherine's eyes. "I'm trying to figure things out."

"You can count on stares from everyone who regards you as a whore. No White man will ever want you again because you've been intimate with a Negro. Your story that you were raped won't seem credible if you keep Isaiah on this plantation. You can be killed if the truth comes out. This is a very complicated situation. I won't be back to talk to you about this again. I've offered my sincere friendship and sound advice as a seasoned woman. Do the right thing. You won't regret it."

ഇ

After Mary left Rutherford Rocks in a buggy just ahead of the crack of dawn, her mind was fixed on stopping to buy fresh buns and knitting. Catherine's mind didn't budge from a big decision that she had to make. She drifted off to sleep while having nightmares of angry White men aiming rifles at the heads of enslaved workers, demanding to know where Isaiah was. In her thoughts, the weakest relented under duress while being forced to enter the plantation doors, march up the winding staircase, and point out the child in his cradle.

"No!" Catherine screamed, imagining the men in the mob snatching her son from her arms. Her mind flashed to scars on Juniper's arms where ropes had dug into his flesh. His dead body hung from a tree. She watched it swing to and fro. A buzzard landed on his shoulder.

Catherine awoke sweating, her heart racing in her chest, eager to run and check on her son.

"Is you okay, Missus?" Rhodie asked, rubbing her eyes.

She slowly stood to her feet, rising from a small bed in Catherine's room.

"Yes. No. I don't know." Catherine picked up her innocent little boy.

"He wuz sleepin' real good. Me, too. What troubles ya?" Rhodie looked up.

Catherine didn't want to discuss her internal conflict with a young enslaved girl. Her hands shook.

"Missus, ya looks like yous done seen a ghost."

Isaiah began to cry. Catherine stared deeply into his eyes and saw the eyes of his father, Juniper. Suddenly, she felt afraid of the baby, nearly dropping him. Rhodie ran to catch the baby as he slipped from Catherine's fingers.

"Missus, do ya need da doctor?"

Catherine backed away, her gaze fixed on the baby. Just as she was about to release a blood-curdling scream, a hand covered her mouth.

14

The Unthinkable

❦⟫⟫⟫⟪⟪⟪❦

Catherine's sister, Sarah Ann, had shown up by mule and wagon like a humble shepherd. As Mary left, Sarah Ann appeared, bringing her sister a glass of water. She spoke to Rhodie after wondering why the child was struggling to carry a brown jug of liquor toward the Great House. After Rhodie explained that it was for Catherine, Rhodie's eyes told Catherine how afraid she was of getting punished.

"Dis here what Aunt Sarah done fixed way back. Been left over from when de big folks had dey celebration. I's takin' it to Missus Catherine right now," Rhodie said.

Sarah Ann shook her head. "Just water will be fine. I'll take it to her."

Rhodie looked confused because both sisters had given her conflicting instructions.

"You have my word. It's okay to leave without taking this, Rhodie," Sarah Ann said with a nod.

Rhodie swallowed hard. "I's gon' get dat water, Missus."

Sarah Ann set foot on the ground she swore she'd never visit unless enslaved people were free. She had become a servant of God who wanted to nurture the lives of others while working as an abolitionist. She regarded oppressed people as worthy of receiving double prosperity for their trouble, just as Job had received in the Bible.

Sarah Ann didn't know what she would learn, but she always had a knack for knowing when her sister was in trouble. So, she prayed for God's direction and headed to the plantation. God told her to show the devotion she'd once shown because Catherine and Sarah Ann's parents were in Heaven. She could not abandon the sister she'd grown up with in her time of need.

When Sarah Ann showed up in the hallway at Rutherford Rocks, she could sense trouble, unrest, and even death. She knew the signs from growing up in the elite planter class. Sarah Ann didn't know what she would see or hear, but she prayed she could withstand it. She pushed her sister's door open without knocking, just as screams began to leave the back of her throat, conjuring nightmares about violent mobs showing up to wreak havoc.

"Nothing is impossible with your help, God," Sarah Ann quietly mumbled.

She placed the water on a table in the hallway. Sarah Ann walked toward her sister, instinctively wanting to protect her by covering her mouth to keep her visit as low-key as possible. Although the sisters had drifted apart, Catherine was glad to see Sarah Ann when she realized it was her.

"No screaming. It's me, Sarah Ann. Quiet your cries."

A flame of hope ignited in Catherine. Sarah Ann removed her hands from her sister's mouth. Catherine's icy thoughts subsided and melted like gentle rain.

"It's you. Thank God."

"I'm not a saint, and I'm here to mend our relationship. I'm here because I know some serious challenges have found your path. What is going on at Rutherford Rocks?"

God's timing was perfect. Catherine needed her sister. She clung to her without words. Through her energy, she cried out to connect with the only sibling who had come to be by her side, once again.

"If you're hugging me, I know things are bad. What have you done?"

Catherine released her sister. "I'm glad you showed up. I need help. I know that we have our issues, but please don't refuse my request."

Sarah Ann glanced across the room. She saw Isaiah in a bassinet. She held her head and inhaled as Catherine silently answered from the depths of her soul.

"Please tell me you didn't—"

Catherine began to wail, but first, Sarah Ann found Rhodie and asked her to take the baby out of the room. This time, she offered Rhodie syrup and cornbread in the kitchen as a treat.

Sarah Ann looked at Catherine. "I need to know everything."

"I've done the unthinkable. I can't tell you everything."

"This is your time of need. You better tell me what you've gotten yourself into. And who did you tell about your situation?"

"Mary."

"Mary Rector, wife of Senator Rector?"

Catherine nodded.

"How could you trust an enemy's kindness in your time of need? That was a big mistake."

"I didn't get the impression that she was an enemy." Catherine hadn't studied Mary that closely when she was holding teacups at lunches and dinner parties.

Sarah Ann divulged pieces of Mary's history. "She and her husband have a reputation for buying up farmland to grow more cotton, but they need more slaves as they expand their operation to increase profit. Mary is known to observe slaves from other plantations since it's illegal to import them now."

Catherine thought of comments Mary made about the attributes of enslaved workers like Aunt Sarah, Rhodie, and even wanting to get rid of Jeremiah. She felt confused since Mary had told her to arrange a private sale of Jeremiah and a few others.

"I can't believe she would trick me and buy my best workers."

"I can intercede on your behalf."

Just as Catherine began to trust her sister, she spotted something around her neck. "I've seen that rabbit's foot before. I know it from someplace."

Sarah Ann was quiet.

"Colored folks think they're good luck. Why would you have one?"

"It was a gift," was all she would say. She didn't want to lie or admit that it had belonged to Aunt Sarah. The woman often kept it with her, but Sarah Ann struggled to recall the origin of Aunt Sarah's charm. She also didn't want to unpack the tale of helping Aunt Sarah escape to Mexico. She prayed that God would let the clue pass by Catherine's over-taxed mind.

She drew her attention back to Catherine, who was divulging details about her situation that had to be carefully managed. Sarah Ann agreed that Isaiah couldn't stay on the plantation. As much as she hated slavery, she helped to craft a plan for Isaiah and any others who would leave Rutherford Rocks with him under the circumstances.

"The sale won't be public. It's the best way to try and avoid disastrous consequences. I guarantee that Mary Rector expects you to show up and put everyone on an auction block in the morning. She'd buy them and destroy you in the process. She wants to have the biggest plantation in the South. I've told you before that slavery should end, not increase."

Catherine decided to listen to Sarah Ann, despite their strained relationship.

"Remember, Isaiah is my nephew. I care about him, too."

After Sarah Ann settled on a plan with her sister, they agreed that the enslaved people would only be sold as a family. The next morning, more household bonds were interrupted at the plantation without public scrutiny.

Catherine felt nauseous and weak when Isaiah left Rutherford Rocks in Rita's arms. Catherine experienced what it felt like when enslaved women were separated from their children. She had sold her own son into slavery, along with ten other slaves, to get out of debt—including Rita and her baby. She suspected that her husband was the father of the youngest baby born at Rutherford Rocks: Titus. She didn't want to think about what he may have done a third time. Her mind was fixed on sweet Isaiah, the enslaved baby who shared her blood.

For the first time in her life, Catherine didn't attend a slave auction where slave dealers looked to buy enslaved people because she wanted her son to leave her arms with all the dignity she could muster under the circumstances. The enslaved group was sold privately without bidding wars by brokerage at Rutherford Rocks. Catherine had once beaten enslaved children. Now, she didn't want Isaiah to be touched or treated like a horse or mule.

"No one better put a scratch on him!" she screamed like a loving mother.

She clung to her baby, feeling desperate, torn, and helpless. Catherine drew a deep breath while trying to calm herself. She thought about how hate was a terrible thing. She had treated enslaved people worse than animals. She had never looked past slavery's chains until now. Countless enslaved families endured the separation of loved ones and suffered because of it. Catherine was reaping what she had sown.

"Let them go. Isaiah cannot stay with you. You must do this to save Isaiah and yourself. He will get by somehow. God knows his story," Sarah Ann whispered into her sister's ear.

Catherine uncurled her fingers from around the little boy, although she couldn't surrender her worries. "Take good care of him, Rita."

Rita said nothing. She was a child with a baby of her own to care for, although Catherine coached her to say Isaiah's mother had died at the plantation in childbirth.

Catherine didn't know how to rebuild her life with a piece of herself gone. She wanted her son to grow up to love his own skin with all of his heart and soul. She wondered how he would develop as a person, if he would miss his mother, or how Rita would discipline him. Catherine knew Rita would not shape him to feel empowered as a dark-skinned Negro male. She resented that Rosalind and Bradley's Whiter and mixed-race appearance granted them certain privileges, even though they were enslaved children.

Catherine quietly requested that her son be showered with blessings and grow up to be successful through God's grace.

Suddenly, enslaved people had souls, intelligence, and feelings. For the first time, she was selling her family to someone else.

As the wagon disappeared down the road, Catherine screamed, cried, and fell to her knees in the dirt. "Isaiah!"

Sarah Ann patted her sister on the back. "I'm sorry."

∽∞∾

When an angry mob showed up at Rutherford Rocks, there was nothing controversial to see. They pushed their way inside the slave quarters looking for Isaiah. All they could find was Fishin' Sam taking a Saturday break near the big oak trees. There was no fussing, fighting, or controversy. Every baby at Rutherford Rocks was a full-blooded Negro. Catherine kept repeating the story that her baby had died, and no other babies had been recently born after she had been raped by Juniper. Sarah Ann was long gone. She had told her sister what to say and how. Catherine took her chances and faced the mob.

"He was hung," she said.

She exhaled deeply after the angry mob turned around and left just after breakfast.

"I knows you's mighty glad dat storm done passed," Rhodie said.

Hazel walked into the parlor with Rosalind and Bradley. "What was all that noise?"

"You are the ones who should've been sold," Catherine snapped.

"Why didn't you do it then?" Hazel challenged.

"I've treated you good because I've known you so long," Catherine said.

Catherine hid her truth. Emptiness returned when John Rutherford smacked her in the face from the grave. She was going to sell Hazel and her children, but there was a legal problem the executor pointed out when she cleaned up business. Massa Brower's will stated that upon his death, Hazel and her children were to be set free. It was illegal for enslaved people to be set free in Alabama, and Catherine was the rightful owner of Hazel, although it was part of Catherine's dowry. Massa left his colored children and Hazel property and money in his will.

"If anyone finds out about this, I'll fight against it in court," Catherine had mumbled.

Catherine didn't have the desire to tell Hazel. She hid the papers in a secret hiding place because she feared that at least one of them could read.

Hazel said, "I's only been good enough for you to hate, blame and beat 'cause of whatever problems you had in private wit' Massa Brower."

Catherine slapped Hazel. "You have such a smart mouth. You've gotten too comfortable for your own good."

"If you need anything, Missus, just let me know," Hazel said humbly.

"Massa's gone now. Return to the slave quarters, you and your children. That's what I need you to do."

Hazel ushered her children to their room to pack quietly. Bradley and Rosalind started to complain, but Hazel quieted them.

"Massa's dead. Missus wants us out of the Great House. Do as I told you to do."

"Massa was my pappy, my family. His blood runs through my veins. Why should I have to go back to the slave quarters?" Rosalind asked.

"Because Missus said so. She was his wife," Hazel explained.

"You don't ever respect Missus. Why should I?" Rosalind asked.

Rosalind's expression showed how lost she was as a mixed-race, enslaved young woman. Not fitting in anywhere left her feeling adrift.

"Neither of you are good at understanding that we are slaves! We have no rights. Missus owns us!" Bradley hollered while bundling up items for their move.

Catherine stood in the doorway. "One more thing. All of you can start working in the fields. Actually, Rosalind and Hazel can. Bradley has more respect for me. I'll move him to an apprenticeship so he can learn a trade." With that, she turned and walked away, leaving them to feel exactly what they were—slaves.

Hazel observed Rosalind's lack of discipline and her unbridled tongue. Hazel wondered how her daughter would fare in a world that would still see her as a Negro. Massa Brower's spoiling had given Hazel and Rosalind inflated egos. The girl wanted to ride in a buggy to the slave quarters. Instead, the trio carried their items, facing a mile-long walk ahead, forced to pursue a changed lifestyle.

15

Can't Keep a Good Man Down

Henry didn't remember what year he had first met Hazel at Rutherford Rocks. It didn't matter to him because seeing Hazel's face would be like making it to Heaven's pearly gates on Earth. All that mattered was that Henry remembered the joy that love had brought him before he was sold to another plantation.

He prioritized Hazel's well-being over the years and never forgot that he wanted to enable her to have a joyful life as a married woman someday. Henry had just installed windows on the north end of his newly constructed home. He was proud of the way construction was shaping up, down to the piles of lumber that were neatly stacked outside the decorative rocks that would line the rose bushes.

"Hazel will like these," he had told Ritchie, a man who was paid to give Henry a hand.

"Who's Hazel?"

"The future lady of the house. I'm doing all of this to make her comfortable."

"This is a mighty fine piece of property you have on your hands. I've never seen a Negro man have a place like this. I reckon that woman must be something special to see."

"She is a real work of art." Henry shook the dirt from his shoes.

He thought of Hazel's high cheekbones, magical dark eyes, and smooth skin with every step he took toward her. After traveling for a few days by foot and train, Henry showed up at the slave quarters, nearly a mile from the Great House, looking for Hazel, the love of his life whom he hadn't seen in almost two decades. Each time he tapped on a door, he looked around the bunks for anyone sleeping, feeling a sense of duty to find his dear Hazel.

When he finally saw someone moving around outside, Henry asked an enslaved worker who was looking after horses and feeding hogs if Hazel had been sold. If he had to go to every cabin in the row, he was ready to do it. Through her relationship with Massa Brower, Hazel learned that such a relationship didn't have to lead to marriage for enslaved women. She'd become hard-hearted and doubtful of whether one was worth having.

Hazel began unpacking her items in the slave quarters where Catherine had told her to go. Rosalind and Bradley left to fetch water. Hazel was glad that it was a Sunday; at least they had the day off. Her work in the fields would start early in the morning. The thought of sleeping on wooden slabs instead of the bed Massa Brower had given her made her stomach sink. Even worse was imagining the clang of a big bell calling families to line up for their weekly food rations. Pork and fatty meat turned her stomach, but at least she still had Juniper's old garden, where she could harvest fresh turnip greens. That was a start.

As she walked that way, sounds of snickering and laughter filled the air.

"Is you fixin' to come to de dance when night falls?" Milly asked.

"What dance?" Hazel asked, holding her greens.

"We's mighty glad to see you back on dis part of de plantation."

Hazel sighed.

"You done thought you and dem chilluns was special to Massa. Well, look what done come of y'all now."

"Stay away from us!"

"I's gonna see you when de sun rise in dem fields. If'n you wants to come to de celebratin', we got plenty banjos and fiddles playin'. Ain't every day dat you and yo' chilluns git what's comin' to ya. Just wait til tomorrow when you out dere in dem fields. De driver gonna show you where you belongs. Don't matter none dat you been Massa Brower's pet darky."

Catherine hadn't hired another overseer. A designated Negro driver had been selected to keep everyone on task or to prevent them from working slowly.

Hazel couldn't believe that her own people could be so cruel. She planned to regroup and prepare to return to the tasks that she hated, but a knock changed her evening plans.

"Milly, I said don't come over here bothering me! Some people don't get what being left alone should mean. You're one of them!" she yelled.

Hazel felt superior to Milly and the enslaved field hands who never set foot in the Great House. She'd eaten fine food when Milly only had small bits of food left to eat. She had slept in a real bed.

The persistent knock made Hazel answer the door. She opened it, feeling prepared to put Milly in her place. It wasn't who she expected.

"Hazel?" the man said, squinting.

"Do I know you?"

"You most certainly do. Take a good look at my face." The man outstretched his arms.

Henry's eyes told a story of someone who wanted to spread kindness and peace, but he didn't get the reception he thought he would. Henry dropped his arms. His hair had a few subtle silver streaks along with some brown. He looked more mature but not far from how he once had.

"I'm sorry, but I don't think I know who you are."

"You haven't hardly aged a bit. Can I have a single conversation with you?"

He was mesmerized by the woman he still loved. Hazel didn't look her age; it was as if God had preserved her just for him.

"We'll see. I already asked who you are."

"It's me. You should know."

"Me who?"

"Henry. Did you expect me to give up easy? When I said I loved you, I meant it. There's no security with a man who won't be willing to fight." He grinned.

Hazel's eyes widened. "Henry who was sent away from Rutherford Rocks?"

"In the flesh!" He wanted to jump up but thought better about it.

Henry embraced Hazel with the strength of his eighteen-year-old self. Hazel couldn't recognize him now because of the time that had passed; Massa Brower had taught her to forget such a beautiful man. Henry spun Hazel around playfully as best he could. Hazel had been brainwashed to believe that she wasn't beautiful. She didn't understand why Henry was making such a big fuss about her. His emotions were pure and genuine. He missed everything small and great about Hazel, from the shape of her knees and lips to the way she made his heart leap when she smiled, but her energy had dulled.

"Put me down. Don't make too much noise. I can't believe my eyes, but I don't want any dogs to be after you," Hazel told Henry, glancing around.

"I need a hug—not the push-away kind, the one where you wrap your arms around me."

Hazel ignored his request.

"You got a pass from your massa to come to Rutherford Rocks?"

Henry didn't need a note permitting him to leave the person he belonged to.

"I don't belong to anyone other than God, Hazel." Henry carefully placed Hazel on her feet.

"Are you sure you're not running away from home?"

"Aren't you going to ask me if I want to come in?"

Hazel stepped aside to allow Henry to enter her cabin. Henry pulled out his freedom papers to prove that he had been emancipated. "I filed with the county deeds office in case something happened to my documents."

Henry feared that a dishonest judge could rule that the papers were fake, but he still took the chance. Slave catchers were known to try to capture free Negroes or destroy their papers. It was worth the risk.

"I'm a free Negro now. I've been a blacksmith. We talked about having a shack. I bought some land. I've been building a better home for us than this. I'm almost finished adding more furniture. I got a beehive so you can have fresh honey. The garden is coming along mighty fine. That's why I came here looking for my queen. You've always been in my prayers. Did you ever wonder about me?"

Hazel looked away. Henry didn't reveal that a Negro slaveholder had initially bought him for benevolent reasons after he had been sold by another master. When Henry noticed that the owner began to buy more enslaved workers and was abusive to them, he fled.

"A woman needs someone she can count on, but so does a man. I'm showing you that I'm responsible and committed." He paused, looking at her. "Why don't you look happy to see me?"

"Maybe I thought everything you said to me was just conversation, 'cause after so many years, I lost count."

"It matters less than a man's heart. If a man loves you, he's gonna show it. I took a big risk coming back here. A slave catcher could frame me, and back to slavery I'd go. I bought my own freedom."

"It ain't your job to save me."

"Why do you talk to me so rough?" He wondered if Hazel had considered the effort and the risks he took to reunite with her.

"Massa kept me well-fed, well-clothed, and he kept a roof over my head when I couldn't even take care of myself. Massa civilized us."

"I got sent away. You remember?"

"It don't matter how; you left me. The point is that you did."

Henry's feelings were hurt. Betrayal, confusion, and pain crowded his mind. Hazel believed that dark skin made Negroes genetically inferior.

"I had to do a whole lot to get here, and this is all you can say?"

"A lot has changed with me over the years." Hazel was unsympathetic.

She didn't want to repeat how Massa Brower stalked and raped her until she loved him more than Henry.

"Over the years, I couldn't shake my love for you from this brain of mine. You kept me motivated to never give up loving you. I didn't take weekends or holidays off to meet our goal of having a house and being together."

"You don't never have a wife?"

"Massa whip me often for stickin' to my principles. A small, skinny Negro like me wasn't expectin' to be good breedin' material. Negroes do better stayin' with their families. Slavery teach us to walk off after makin' a room full of chilluns. I try to use my brain and be better than dat."

Hazel realized that she'd picked a good man many years ago when she and Henry first shared a kiss in their secret nook. She began to question her loyalty and love for Massa Brower. Hazel wept.

"What's wrong with you, gal?"

Henry sensed that the words Hazel spoke felt like a strange dance after everything that had happened to split them up. Henry wanted to feel the enthusiasm young Hazel had. This new Hazel seemed uninspired and complacent.

"You seem like a real good man, that's all."

"Then why you treat me so cold and mean?" Henry moved closer to taste Hazel's lips.

Hazel jumped when Bradley and Rosalind entered the cabin, talking loudly as they carried water from the spring.

"Who's he?" Rosalind asked.

"Henry. Say hello."

Her children were evidence of the disruption of a normal family unit. Their master was their father, and he was dead. Hazel didn't want to introduce her children to the plantation.

"It's nice to meet you, Mr. Henry. My sister and I will be moving along now," Bradley said.

"I don't want to go anywhere," Rosalind complained.

Bradley tugged at her arm. "We have more chores to do."

When the door shut, Hazel backed away. "I have something to tell you."

"I'm listening."

"I's been with Massa Brower since you left. He's dead now, but I did da best I could. I couldn't make him leave me alone. I's got two chillun by him. I's sorry, Henry." Tears streamed down her face.

Henry felt that his years of fighting to be a gentleman were for nothing. "We used to be so close."

Hazel wanted to resent the children that she had with Massa Brower and all the things he made her do before they were born, for a single moment. But playing the wife made her feel that she was in a noncommitted relationship. She didn't want to regard Massa Brower as a rapist. The callous woman who was unable to deal with her own trauma had become the mother of her innocent children.

"They need you. Slave women don't have any control or legal protection, I suppose. That means what happened ain't your fault."

"You forgive me?"

She knew she was too old to have more children. If she had a choice, Henry would have been the father of the new lives she brought into the world as her loving husband.

"It's not the news I wanted to hear, but seeing you still feels like Christmas morning."

Hazel slowly took three steps toward Henry. She pressed her lips against his. Pain turned to pleasure, as sweet as nectar from a honeysuckle plant that grew on a vine at Rutherford Rocks. This time, she didn't allow Massa Brower's memory to affect her chance to taste Henry's lips.

"Take back your mind. Don't you let the kind of love we have die," Henry whispered.

Hazel's hard shell melted when Henry gently kissed her again.

Nodding, Hazel agreed. "I reckon you're right. Let's take a walk."

The pair walked past the spring where they used to get water together. They stopped at a patch of grass and an oak tree where they first professed their love for each other. Henry kissed Hazel's lips again when he recognized the big tree where they had shared their happiest moments on a day of rest. Hazel looked at Henry, finally realizing that Massa Brower had taken everything from her—her love, her marriage, and her children with the right man. She felt angry enough to say words she never thought she would.

"I hope Massa Brower rot in hell for what he did taking away the love of my life," Henry said.

"Don't talk about the dead so disrespectfully."

"I'm not gon' change my way of expression because Brower is dead. He won't a good man. Brower regarded you, me, and all the slaves as subhuman."

Hazel tried to ignore Henry's bitterness as they sat on the grass. The ground felt like it had in their youth.

"Children are a blessing. If God didn't want 'em to be, they wouldn't have been born."

"Your husband finally here, if ya still want him." Henry smiled.

"I can't come with you." Hazel started feeling dizzy.

"Maybe later. I'm willing to wait a lifetime if I must. And that boy of yours is gon' need a man to teach him how to be a man. A woman can't do that the same way."

Bradley didn't have a grandfather or uncle to be an example for him. Hazel knew that Henry had a good point. She didn't want to acknowledge his perceptiveness, so she changed the topic.

"I guess true love never dies. It shows forgiveness, patience, and it pure," Hazel reasoned.

"Sumthin' like dat," Henry agreed.

"I wonder what life could be like for me with you if I was free."

Henry lifted his shirt to show Hazel his back. "This happened last time I laid eyes on you. These marks—these scars came because I wouldn't allow Massa Brower to tell me who to love. That was you."

"So now it was my fault?"

Henry spotted a broom. He laid it down and joined hands with Hazel. "You know how much I love you, so would you?"

"I's not jumping the broom with you."

Henry was disappointed that their joyous memory was not made, but he only wanted a wife who wanted a husband just as much. He watched Hazel wash clothes and let them dry by the fire. Candlelight made Henry's skin radiant. It glowed softly.

"Give time a chance. I'll come back for you. I know one day things will get better. Maybe I can buy your freedom. We'll take things slow."

He didn't tell Hazel that he was already prepared to pay one thousand dollars to make it possible. Hazel wished she could run away to the woods and enjoy being married, but Catherine had authority over her. She wondered if Henry would help raise Rosalind and Bradley. Would Henry share land with them? Hazel had heard of other children of the plantation who had a hard time in life being accepted by either part of their heritage. They looked nothing like Henry. She imagined that Henry's pain would be too much for him to accept her children. It would be a constant reminder that Massa Brower had his way with her. Hazel's loyalty stayed with Rosalind and Bradley. She knew that she would be a single parent.

"You were set free, but I will die rememberin' the problems of a slave who never had a right to have a proper wedding and husband."

"What do you want?"

"The battle to love is ova. I quit."

Hazel hadn't bothered to utter one kind word to Henry. She stood up from the grass and began walking back toward the cabin. Hazel wasn't the same person anymore. She found it hard to keep her emotions in a positive place. Even if enslaved people gossiped that Massa Bower was the one who had impregnated her, no one dared to discuss it. Catherine's turn to mistreat Hazel and her children had arrived. The tables had turned when Massa Brower died. Hazel knew she had gone too far by loving a married man who had a legal right to control her every move, yet somehow Hazel managed to blame Henry for having children with her oppressor.

Henry stood to follow Hazel. "How can you quit on something that is good for you? All I've done is show that I mean what I said. I love you from the bottom of my heart."

"Too much has happened. I don't care 'bout lovin' you no more."

"A man shows up at Rutherford Rocks looking to make good on promises and dreams, and that's all you have to say?" Frustrated, Henry stood with one hand on his hip, shaking his head. "You been brainwashed to believe that Massa Brower saw you as a woman. Really, he tore out ya soul, ya childhood and innocence."

Henry couldn't believe that an aging Hazel had been convinced to forget the horrors of being deemed property. Somehow, she forgot that she had begun working as an enslaved child at the age of five. Then, Massa Brower first produced a child of rape before Hazel willingly complied with his wishes.

"I can't believe what I'm hearing."

Hazel looked at him. "There's one mo' thing."

"Whatchu got?" Henry followed Hazel to the front of her cabin.

"Don't come back, Henry, at least not for me."

"Massa Brower makes babies with you, don't provide for 'em 'cause he don't legally have to, but you're mad at me."

"Why insult a dead man? Massa Brower took care of all his slaves for many years. Be respectful."

Henry frowned, unable to process how she had cast his faithfulness aside. The number of White men who fathered children on the plantation angered him, yet these men faced no judgment for creating broken homes or for abandoning their children. No one seemed to mention the damage they did to the innocent children they fathered.

"John Brower ain't my master. I owe half a man nothing— not from his grave or when he was in my face in the flesh! He destroyed our love, and you talk about him like he was the most moral man walkin'. Everything you did was on his terms."

Henry didn't want to waste all of his blessings on himself. He hadn't told Hazel that he'd bought one hundred acres of land that he had been farming on. He brought in a profitable income and had a large home on the grounds. After he paid for his freedom, he refused to be underpaid but overworked.

Hazel huffed, offended by the truth. "Massa Brower didn't allow Missus to sell me or my chillun. She wanted to send my gal to another plantation when she was born. He said naw."

Henry clapped sarcastically. "That don't mean he loved you. He was drawn to you 'cause he could snatch your dignity and body wit' no complaints from anybody important enough to stop him."

"You can crack jokes if ya want to but no one wants to struggle wit' a darkie who don't have any learnin'. Massa's been good to me. Such a great man just gone. I known him for many years. Home is right here at Rutherford Rocks and I don't need you or the little bit you pretend you got goin' on."

"Fasten your slick tongue! I'm jus' a man who loves a woman. Hate is a language I don't speak. I would die for you, but you have no right to treat me like you trying to take my sanity."

"You don't own me! I'm all grown."

"I'm tryin to bring back the togetherness we lost as loyal friends 'cause of slavery and you don't give me no credit for that. But you never once held our old massa morally responsible for what he done to you. My sweet Hazel called me a darkie. I never thought I'd hear you talk about me that way. You're making the mistake of your life. You can't keep a good man down, but I won't argue to prove how hard I worked to become a better man."

Massa Brower had used his influence and power to poison Hazel's mind. She no longer believed Negro love had a place in her life, but the same White man who had given her things was the same one who took other things away. Henry felt as if he had done enough. His job was not to convince Hazel that he was a valuable blessing.

After living with Brower as an unofficial family unit in the Great House, Hazel became fond of Massa Brower. He grew emotionally attached to the same people he owned. Brower had trained Hazel to obediently cohabitate with him as a mistress. She distanced herself from male slaves and couldn't find it in herself to express love to Henry as she once had.

The pair didn't push to finish the conversation. Henry kept asking himself what he had done to deserve the harsh treatment he received. A woman in his own race, who shared a similar background, discriminated against him with brutal hatred. Hazel watched Henry turn around to walk down the road. When Henry looked back at her, it felt like the stars fell from the sky and broke.

Henry was taught not to cry so he didn't, although he wished he could.

"I, I—" Hazel stuttered.

She couldn't release "I love you" from her lips. She did love him but couldn't admit what her heart felt; Henry was the best man she ever had.

16

Good Vibes

❖➤➤➤ ❮❮❮❖

Catherine knelt on the cold, uneven ground, her black mourning dress pooling around her in the damp earth. The thick air smelled of turned soil, the distant rustle of the wind the only sound beyond her quiet breaths. Before her stood John Brower's fresh-carved headstone, its stark simplicity a testament to the time and the haste of its erection.

"This wasn't what I planned." Her voice cut through the stillness like the sharp edge of a blade. Her gloved hands rested in her lap, fingers trembling against the lace trim of her veil. The words felt bitter on her tongue, but they needed to be spoken—to him, to the world, to herself.

"Thanks to your undisciplined behavior, I'm a widow." She spat the last word, her gaze fixed on the grave as though daring it to argue back. Her bonnet tipped as she bowed her head, the sheer veil doing little to hide the redness around her eyes or the flush of her cheeks from the chill.

A lone horse-drawn carriage rattled by in the distance, its wooden wheels creaking against the frozen dirt road. The sound faded, leaving only the whisper of the wind. Catherine reached for the small bouquet she had brought—wildflowers gathered in haste from the side of the Great House.

"Was it worth it, John?" she whispered, her voice softer now, almost pleading. Her shoulders slumped beneath the heavy weight of her shawl, the perfect picture of grief shadowed by anger.

Catherine placed the flowers on the grave. She lingered for a moment, her gloved fingers brushing the rough edges of the stone. The coolness seeped through the fabric, grounding her in the grim reality of her loss.

When she rose, her skirt rustling against the grass, she adjusted her bonnet and straightened her spine. Overwhelmed and drained, a tear traced her rosy cheek as she contemplated the flesh she'd traded for wealth and the countless women Massa Brower had bedded at Rutherford Rocks. Her whisper fell soft as twilight air.

"The money doesn't even matter anymore. This is all your fault. You left me with a mess on my hands. You had children by Hazel. I had to give up my baby, and I never had the security of having one of your offspring. I'll never forgive you for giving a Negro woman something you didn't even give your wife."

She wondered if Massa Brower had impregnated Hazel on purpose or if fate had struck twice. Though she had raised enough money through slave sales to cover Rutherford Rocks' debts and final loan, profit no longer salved her brokenness. She spat upon her husband's grave, her spirit too weary to rule the plantation.

She walked to a jutting stone near the slave quarters. Her gaze swept the slave cemetery until it settled on an unmarked grave. She knelt, folding her hands in prayer as momentary guilt pierced her conscience. Instead of a proper funeral, they had dug a hole and cast dirt upon it, as though the life beneath meant nothing—neither mother nor daughter.

Catherine had stolen Rhodie's innocence and youth. While Catherine had never swept her own kitchen floor, Rhodie's mother, Phoebe, had perished too soon, collapsing from thirst amid the towering crops under the merciless sun. The sounds of labor drowned out her final plea for water. She had crumpled like a wilting flower, mustering only enough strength for one word: "Help."

Rhodie, born just a week before her mother's death, remained innocent of the system's true brutality, her spirit still malleable as clay.

With her head tilted back, Catherine looked upward. "I'm not in the mood to rule slaves at this plantation. God, I'm beginning to wonder if Sarah Ann was right about slavery being morally wrong."

"Missus, where you been? Did you slip off to say a lil prayer askin' God to make ya path straight?" Rhodie smiled.

Catherine startled. "You shouldn't be here."

"Why? I already feed the chickens and de pigs before I come ta look for you. I hope we don' kill no hogs soon. They act so sweet, Missus. Let dem live."

Catherine yearned to tell Rhodie of the beautiful light that emanated from her but could not bring herself to compliment an enslaved girl who had never known the comfort of shoes.

"I's keeps watchin' how you sufferin', how yo' spirit troubled. Life done dragged you through de mud. Dat must be why you keeps drinkin' from dead Massa's bottles. Do dat ease de pain in yo' heart? I loves you true, Missus. De Lawd knows we all got good and bad in us. But I's feared you gonna kill yo'self wit dat drinkin'. What's gonna happen to dis po' chile if de only friend I's got leaves dis world?" Rhodie embraced Catherine.

Tears burst forth as emotion flooded Catherine's heart. Her life lay in ruins around her, yet here stood Rhodie offering kindness. She held the girl in silence until finally whispering, "Please forgive me, Rhodie."

"For what, Missus?"

"Everything. I haven't been good to you and you still are pouring out praise." Catherine sniffed.

"De Lawd bless yo' heart, Missus. Ain't nobody I trust but you. Let me cook you up some chicken stew wit' dem noodles you likes. When you gets some good vittles in yo' stomach, things ain't gon' seem so heavy on yo' mind."

Catherine brushed the dark soil from her hands, the earth's grit a reminder of all she had buried.

"Who dat coming on dem horses?" Rhodie pointed toward the horizon where dust clouds rose.

"Soldiers." Catherine looked up at the approaching riders silhouetted against the sky.

The boom of cannons shattered the air around them.

"I heard the Northern folks and the Southern folks are figthin'. Is dem White folks with pistols and blue coats wit' large brass buttons de Yankees sent by Abe Lincoln?"

The riders drew nearer, their uniforms now visible.

Catherine sighed, drawing herself up straight. "I think so."

The Yankees had already slain four Rebels who attempted to block their advance. Now they poured across Rutherford Rocks' grounds like floodwaters breaking a levee. Catherine trembled like an autumn leaf, wishing she possessed the power to vanish into thin air. She could only stand and watch as her world crumbled around her.

17

Liberty

❖≫≫≪≪❖

The light illuminated the sky at Rutherford Rocks. The work horn had blown for the last time on December 6, 1865, in the United States. This time, the horns did not signal workers to get their workday started. Chattel slavery had been abolished. The 13th Amendment was officially part of the U.S. Constitution during the Civil War.

Venus Brower waved her hands and hollered with tears in her eyes at "the blue jackets" who were also known as Yankees. "I's finally free now!"

The Yankees hollered from their horses that enslaved people were free.

"I done knowed dis was comin'! Praise de Lawd, praise de Lawd! My heart 'bout to burst wit' joy at dis blessed news!" Venus spun in circles atop the plush grass.

Venus had always had deep faith. She felt that one day, she would shed the pain of slavery and experience liberation. Her belief in God was strong enough to believe that He would not allow her to sleep on rags in a corner and work in what she called the boiling sun for free until she drew her last breath like her mother, Sadie. When her mother died, Catherine put her back to work in the fields. Venus was not allowed to see her one last time. Venus already thought about changing her name since the Brower family didn't own her anymore. Venus began to pack her things at record speed. She had no plan for a place to go, but she was ready to put life at Rutherford Rocks behind her.

"I's gon' be able ta go ta school like free folks and learn my letters and writin'!"

The emancipation of the plantation's enslaved people released a torrent of emotion, from the oldest to the youngest who understood their imminent, unprepared departure. Venus was tired of homemade clothes and not being able to speak her mind. She embraced the chance to live her life with hope.

When Rhodie saw Catherine running from the Yankees toward the Great House, she watched the woman run with the urgency of an enslaved person trying to escape a horrible death. The Yankees kicked up dust with their horses. They shot at Catherine's barrel of molasses and scared the chickens. They let animals walk free from their cages. The horses ran in circles.

"What's all dis here fussin' about?" A man ran toward the Great House.

"We free!" Venus screamed. "Slavery gone!"

"Whatchu saying, gal?" the man asked.

Venus pointed to the Yankees who were destroying Catherine's property that could put money in her pocket. Catherine ran to grab her gold and silver inside of the Great House. She flung open a drawer in her bedroom and grabbed random pieces from all around the house. A few small items had been buried outside of the woods, which Catherine had hidden when she heard about what Abraham Lincoln was trying to do. She didn't believe a day of freedom would really come for enslaved workers, so she was ill-prepared.

Heading to the woods, Catherine tried to recall where her secret spot was to hide her valuables. Acorns covered the land. She dropped everything that she carried when she heard the Yankees charging her way on horseback, firing shots into the air.

"Don't kill me!" Catherine ran to the tree where Massa had hanged Juniper. "Lord, just take me now!"

Catherine threw herself down in the dirt, curling into a ball. A group of Yankees surrounded her. They snatched her valuables, stripping her of her material possessions.

One cocked a pistol and pointed it at her. He wore a blue cap atop his head. "These Negroes are as free as you are now. Am I clear?"

Catherine shook and cried in the dirt, feeling sorry that she had done her own bossing of slaves without hiring another overseer. Owning enslaved people wasn't a woman's job or right.

A lump formed in Catherine's throat when she thought of Sarah Ann's warning that slavery would be the country's downfall. The Yankee pointing the pistol at her had death in his eyes. She finally forced a response, her voice shaking.

"Yes, I know they're all free as I am," she cried out.

Catherine felt as unprotected as a free dog. The Yankees turned around on their horses and left her alone. They took whatever they wanted, including good things to eat. Catherine sobbed, eying the stump where Juniper climbed to his death before he was unjustly lynched.

"Lord, forgive me for my sins!"

She stood up without even bothering to smooth her hair or shake the dirt from her long skirt. Catherine climbed onto the top of the stump. The rope was still intact. She slid her head inside the noose, and a spirit of death seized her mind.

When Catherine began to step from the sawed-off tree, someone yelled, "Stop, Missus! Don't get down!"

Catherine froze. She didn't really want to die; she just wanted the pain to stop. Catherine snapped out of her suicidal daze when Bradley ran up to her. He climbed onto the stump to remove the rope from around her neck.

"God don't want your life to end this way. Neither do I."

They stepped off the stump. When Catherine realized her husband's son, whom she hated, had saved her life, she realized how wrong she'd been.

He wiped his eyes with his fingers. "It's gon' be all right."

Catherine hugged him. "I don't deserve to live."

"If God didn't want you here, you'd already be dead."

Catherine released Bradley, realizing he'd been born to do many things, including save her life.

"You gotta stick around and do everything God wants you to do first."

Catherine realized he was profound and wise at just eight years old.

Slavery made some people think smarter for survival; Bradley was one of them.

ɪᴏᴄɪ

Rhodie wasn't fond of the Yankee's message. She cried and clung to a mule for hours, struggling to feel a spark of love and hope in the world. "I's frightened deep down in my soul. Ain't got no mammy or pappy. Where's a po' chile like me gonna go?"

She got up and walked to the place that gave her the most comfort. She thought of the days cooking alongside Aunt Sarah, after hauling supplies from the cook's shed. The smart little girl knew that she was an orphan, but Rutherford Rocks was the only home she'd always known.

She peeked around the corner and could see Negroes shaking hands and hugging. She held a cast-iron skillet that Aunt Sarah had handed her while preparing a grand meal for a dinner party.

"Me—Rhodie, don't gots nobody."

Then Rhodie remembered that Aunt Sarah had left behind children, too. She left the cook's shed to find them. Maybe they were having the same fears about their journey.

18

A New Beginning

◊≫≫≪≪◊

It was getting late when Mary Rector showed up to check on Catherine.

"I have a business proposal. I'd like to buy Rutherford Rocks. I'll be fair with the price, and the government is going to pay up to three hundred dollars per slave lost under the District of Columbia Compensated Emancipation Act in the District of Columbia. Former slave owners have to state their loyalty to the Union, though. Imagine if we were able to get paid for setting free our slaves—I mean, freed workers." Mary laughed.

Catherine peered at her. "I don't think it's funny that people like us would get reparations, but the people who were victims get no help."

"So now you're on their side? What happened to the woman who had one of the niggers lynched because of a lie?"

Catherine regretted what she had told Mary about Juniper. "I don't know what you're talking about."

Mary moved about the parlor, smiling. "Of course you don't. I'm sure you forgot that the father of your child died screaming."

"I don't want anything to do with the memories of slavery."

"And why would that be if you became wealthy from it?"

"Because God has been good to me. I narrowly escaped the Yankees burning this place to the ground. Why does everything have to be about who is Black or who is White? Humans are humans."

"I'm usually a good judge of character. I thought we thought alike, and I thought we had mutual admiration for each other."

Catherine smirked. "In some ways, we used to."

"Used to?"

"Mary, do you ever ask God for forgiveness because you owned slaves?"

"You are stressing me out." Mary rubbed her temples. "It's not my fault that their leaders sold their own people to European traders and exchanged textiles, firearms, and alcohol for their rivals. I didn't even exist in the fifteenth century."

"Our slaves didn't exist then either."

Mary's back straightened. "I'm not here to debate with you. Do you want to sell Rutherford Rocks or not?"

"Let me think it over. I don't want to make a hasty decision under the circumstances."

"Don't waste my time. I have other offers to make to serious sellers."

Catherine had already saved money and regained her wealth. She would never have to work again.

"Would you rather shutter the plantation's doors? Just remember that you can't afford to pay for labor to run it all because the Thirteenth Amendment permanently abolished slavery."

"It seems like you've given this quite a bit of thought. Why would you want to take on the burden? And who told you what my financial status is?"

"I have a plan, and the time to act has come. It's as simple as that."

"Are you sure greed has nothing to do with this?"

"Why does motive matter to you? I'm starting to feel unwelcome here. Don't think about my offer too long, or you'll miss the window of opportunity."

Mary was the kind of woman who would get mad about almost anything. Despite being kept waiting when she was ready to make a move, Mary did not divulge her motive to buy Rutherford Rocks. She had life insurance policies out on her slaves because hazardous work took a number of them inside coal mines, but after President Abraham Lincoln issued the Emancipation Proclamation on January 1, 1863, she and her husband planned on more ways to grow their enterprise. Their enslaved workers in the Confederacy escaped to the Union Army behind Union lines. Buying Rutherford Rocks would help Mary and her husband multiply their wealth another way. Her Plan B was sharecropping on three plantations and importing cotton to Britain. She knew she had to offer a price as low as India, Brazil, and Egypt to make it work. Her husband, Senator Rector, already had the right connections. Tom knew that the price of plantation land would drop quickly. They planned to buy land throughout the South to pass on wealth to their children, their children's children, and so on. Land values would return someday. Mary Rector was shrewd and forward-thinking.

ॐ

That night there was singing, banjo playing, dancing, fiddle playing, and brandy drinking in the slave quarters. The next morning, no one stirred on their own. The night ended with laughing and talking shortly before darkness turned to dawn.

Mary Rector returned to Rutherford Rocks, sidesaddle on a horse alongside two brawny men who were there to enforce whatever she said if they were needed. Mary got down and strutted around in her long skirt with a plume sticking out of the right side of her hat, like an emperor of her own land. She rang a big bell to get everyone's attention.

"Now that the big party's over, it's time to get back to reality. You dreamed of being free, but did you ever stop to think that there will be no more free pounds of meat for you helpless critters? Today is your last free ride living in the slave quarters and being taken care of. You have had it good. Real good. And you haven't appreciated the blessings that you've been given. While you all are singing and dancing, have you thought of how you'll survive?"

Mary instilled fear in the freed Negroes, who still had no way of taking care of themselves. Mary hadn't accounted for the ancestral guidance that freed Negroes inherited from Africa. The most spiritually connected formerly enslaved workers leaned on God and the strength of spirits that lived within them to remove obstacles and clear a path for them in the most trying times.

"Freedom has a price that none of you have the money to pay. You'll need to survive and work, but no one is coming to save a penniless people. The Negro race has been set up to fail. All you have is freedom, but resources remain unaddressed."

Smiles turned to frowns as Mary laid bare the harsh reality of racism. She knew she could still profit off their backs without having to bend over herself.

"Who's you ta tell us anything?" Uncle Rufus asked.

"Catherine is selling Rutherford Rocks to me. I'm going to be the new owner. I've come to warn you: not one of you will take advantage of me like you did her. I hope you enjoyed your last bellyful of food on the plantation's tab. You won't be able to live in the past. Starting now, you'll be responsible for taking care of yourselves."

"Where we gon' go?" Venus asked.

"That's your problem, not mine. For those of you who choose to leave, I hope you starve to death. Those who want to stay—we can work out an arrangement. You'll work plots of land that you'll rent from me. I'll take a portion of your crop sales as payment. I'll let you live here and provide tools and seeds on credit—with interest. There will be overseers, contracts, and records. Otherwise, you can pay me cash outright to rent the land. I'll teach you my way of doing things."

"I read about sharecropping on some papers. Nobody wants to stay with you and eat your crumbs as if we haven't suffered enough," Rosalind said boldly.

"And I don't want you here anyway. You think you're better than the others because of your high yellow skin? You might think your pappy gave you a great gift with that bright skin, but your mammy can take her bastard children and leave today! You three have been nothing but trouble!"

Rosalind stepped closer to Mary, stopping just an arm's length away. Owners had taught the enslaved people not to look their enslavers in the eye, but Rosalind held her head high. Her words hit like bullets. Some believed Rosalind had an easier life because of her mixed-race heritage and golden complexion, but in truth, neither the Negro nor White communities fully accepted her. Other Negroes on the plantation accused her of acting superior, while Whites like Catherine saw her as arrogant.

"How can you sleep at night? My brother and I exist because our mother was forced into a relationship with our father. It's not our fault if women like you and Catherine couldn't control your husbands."

"Get out!" Mary hollered.

Rosalind smiled, knowing she had struck a nerve. Mary didn't want the freed Negroes to think too deeply about their exploitation.

Bradley, Rosalind's brother, shook his head, exasperated by her unbridled tongue. "Now look what you done. Why can't you ever just stop talking?"

Rosalind slowly backed away from Mary. "It will be my pleasure to leave this evil place."

She had spent too many nights poring over dusty books in John Brower's study. Although reading and writing had been forbidden, she had learned and excelled. Rosalind was bright but careless. Despite her education and higher social status, she rarely considered the consequences of her bold words. Bradley, in contrast, preferred working with his hands. He felt disappointed that freedom had stolen his chance to fully train as a blacksmith. The weight of being the only boy in his family burdened him heavily.

Hazel, meanwhile, regretted shooing Henry away. She knew he would have come back for her if she hadn't insulted his loyalty. Now she had no one, no backup plan, and no way to care for her two mixed-race children. She hadn't even thought to ask where Henry lived, leaving her vulnerable and alone.

"Meet me at the slave quarters. Planning starts immediately," Mary ordered.

She began at the first shack, opening the door. Two men with visible guns in holsters stood behind her.

"Here I is," the person inside said.

"Are you staying or going?" Mary asked.

"Going."

"Pack now. The rest of your possessions will be disposed of by sunset."

"Yes, Missus." The newly freed person scrambled to pack as Mary moved on to the next shack.

Mary decided to allow orphaned children to stay and work in exchange for room and board. Rhodie, however, knew staying would bring no personal development. She didn't trust Mary Rector and yearned for education and better living conditions. Quietly, Rhodie slipped away, pocketing a few biscuits before heading down the road.

Miss Betsy noticed Rhodie alone. "You can come along wit' us and our little ones." Miss Betsy remembered how Rhodie had shared food with her hungry children, and she admired the girl's willingness to help others.

"De Lawd done planted somethin' special in yo' spirit— you got de makin's of a leader even as a young'un. Don't never let nobody steal dat gift de Good Lawd put inside you," Aunt Sarah had once told Rhodie.

"Yes, ma'am." Rhodie had smiled.

Though she missed Aunt Sarah and even Catherine, Rhodie knew she would be safer in a group.

Rhodie nodded with a smile. "Much obliged, Miss Betsy."

Miss Betsy patted Rhodie's head, accepting her as family. She saw this act of kindness as a testament to her faith that God would care for them all.

Meanwhile, Hazel faced the consequences of her past actions. Once, she had betrayed other enslaved people to curry favor with the Browers. Now, those same people shunned her.

"Where ya headed?" she asked Sadie sweetly.

"Don't know. What it matter ta you? Now Massa dead, you wanna be 'mong Negroes? Keep yo trouble to yuself." Sadie's reply was cold.

Hazel hung her head as Moses reminded her of her sins. "You was out here in de fields wit' de hoe 'fore you had dat first chile. Den you went and turned traitor, tellin' Massa 'bout Charlie tryin' to run. Dem bloodhounds tore my boy to pieces 'cause of yo' loose tongue. We was s'posed to be family to each other."

Hazel had no response. Guilt and regret consumed her as she gathered her children. They were penniless, rejected, and lost. Hazel's only thought was to visit John Brower's grave. Gripping his headstone, she prayed for guidance.

"These children are still yours. You left nothing for me to take care of them."

Hazel's desperation grew as the aftermath of war loomed large. Her journey for survival had only begun.

19

The Showdown

Catherine felt as lonely as a woman standing in the middle of the Red Sea. After living a catered existence, she was driven to prioritize family and love for her Negro son over money. She hadn't given up on finding Isaiah; her son deserved a chance to feel good about himself. Catherine had a mother and father in her home and felt guilt-ridden about participating in parental apathy. It was her fault that Isaiah's biological father couldn't be a role model to him. She wondered if he had to beg for food or hugs. Worry took hold of her morning, noon, and night since her son left Rutherford Rocks in a wagon. She knew there was damage to undo if there was any hope left at all.

"What do you mean Isaiah isn't here anymore?" Catherine spoke to the owner of Sandy Acres Plantation, where she was told that formerly enslaved individuals from Rutherford Rocks had been taken.

"Rita couldn't take care of two babies at once. Sandy Acres was not a large plantation, and no one was available to give a baby attention. Isaiah's mother had died at the plantation in childbirth. There are ten free Negroes here," George Barksdale said.

"Where's Rita?"

"You do know that slavery ended, right? Rita is wherever she wants to be. She left. Everyone left. I'm here trying to figure out how I will survive myself now." He then remembered, "But one thing though—a woman named Mary Rector bought that little boy in a private sale from me. I forgot about that. You've seen one of them; you've seen them all. I don't know why so many of you are concerned about that *one*."

"What is that supposed to mean?" Catherine furrowed her brow.

"Why are you asking about that little Negro boy, anyway? He's nobody special."

"According to you!"

"What's the big deal about him?"

"Worry about your own affairs. I know that you have problems of your own. Thank you kindly for the helpful information. I'll be going now." Catherine walked away with a lump in her throat.

Catherine angrily rode her horse to the Rector Plantation in search of Isaiah. She banged on the front door. Mary answered it.

"I didn't expect to see you today. Are you ready to sell Rutherford Rocks?"

"Where's my Isaiah? I know he's here."

"I never said he wasn't. You didn't ask where Isaiah was the last time I saw you. He wasn't here then. Things change. He was sold to me."

"Why would you buy my son? Why?"

Mary squinted. "If you loved him and wanted him, Isaiah's mammy never would've put him on the wagon to be sold."

"You gave me the idea. It was you." Catherine finger-poked her in the chest.

"I did. You seemed flustered and confused. I did what any good friend would do and pointed out your options to sort out a very sticky problem you had on your hands." Mary grinned.

"Get my boy. I want to see him now!" Catherine pushed Mary.

Mary pushed her back. "That's no way to get what you want. You come into my home, putting your hands on me and making demands as if I must comply, and you believe I have to listen. Shame on you. I thought your mother raised you to be a mannerly Southern Belle."

Catherine stepped on her left foot. "I'm not playing with you."

"And I'm not playing with you. I want Rutherford Rocks."

Catherine balled her fists. "I don't trust you. Is Isaiah here or not?"

"*Isaiah!* Bring Missus Rector her favorite boots!"

A barefoot little boy emerged with Mary's boots. He looked exactly like Catherine, only his complexion was different. He looked skinny, underfed, and barely clothed in a long shirt.

"What's wrong with him?" Catherine asked, shaking.

"That'll be all. Go upstairs," Mary quickly hollered at Isaiah. "And nothing is wrong with my houseboy, Catherine. Mind your business."

"You can't make me. He is my business."

Catherine ran up the steps after Isaiah. He was afraid and ran faster. "I don't want to hurt you. It's me. Your mammy."

Isaiah bolted behind a door and locked it. "Ain't so! You's a White lady! I don't knows you!"

Tom Rector emerged from his home office. "What's going on around here? Who are you and why are you upstairs?"

"I'm Catherine Brower. Your wife took my child."

"Isaiah's a little Negro. Woman, you must be mad!"

Mary Rector appeared, pointing at Catherine. "I want Rutherford Rocks, and I want it now."

"Mary, what is going on here?"

"Let me handle this. Stay out of it, please," she said, whispering something into her husband's ear. His stance changed. "Catherine, we have an iron-clad contract. Sign it or leave. If you choose to sell your property, Isaiah can go."

Mary folded her arms. Catherine's legs weakened. She wobbled and then fell into a wall. After regaining her footing, she forced herself not to panic.

"Fine! But my lawyer will need to review it first."

Tom stood his stance. "Two hours. Take it or leave it."

"I'll be back with him. Get Isaiah ready to go!" She hurried down the steps.

Catherine's lawyer met with Tom and Mary to discuss Rutherford Rocks' future, helping Catherine make an informed decision. Her lawyer wanted to know why she was so driven to protect Isaiah, but Catherine wouldn't divulge her coveted secret. When he heard her refer to the boy as her son, he assumed she had gotten attached to him on the plantation because he was a servant.

"How could you use them to sharecrop and create another oppressive structure when they've just been freed? I don't want to sell Rutherford Rocks to you without a clause being written in that the land won't be used for that purpose."

"You can't tell me what to do when it becomes mine. You don't want Isaiah bad enough, and I've already told all of them at Rutherford Rocks that I would be the new owner."

"You did what?"

"When I see something I want, I move. I told you that about myself a while ago."

"What are you going to do?" Tom Rector asked.

Catherine looked at her lawyer.

"It's all up to you," he told her.

"Hurry up. I must pick out a dress for a wedding I'm attending. I don't have all day."

"Give me the pen."

John invited Catherine and her lawyer into his office to sit down. Catherine reviewed the document one final time. She suddenly saw the potential in all children through the eyes of her own child, regardless of color or how they were born. Catherine took a deep breath and signed the document.

"I won't hand it over until Isaiah is here."

Mary stood and returned with the little boy. He seemed timid and afraid.

Catherine opened her arms. "Come to me, Isaiah."

He shook his head. Catherine felt sorry that she had profited from slavery, but she hadn't yet acknowledged that reaping and sowing were real principles. Sarah Ann cultivated good blessings because she finally acknowledged the principle with a clean heart. Now, Catherine's own son didn't know or trust her.

Mary walked over to the timid child. "Would you like a piece of candy or pound cake?"

The little boy gleefully nodded while feeling less threatened. Mary returned with an assortment of treats. "I'll only let you have it if you go with her in a buggy. Her name is Catherine Brower. Your new missus will explain the rest when she takes you home."

Catherine slowly handed the paper to Tom as her son walked toward her. Tom took it from her grasp as Isaiah took the treats from Mary. The woman handed them to Catherine. Her son finally relented, walking her way. She handed a piece of candy to him and then pressed his small head inside her arms.

"I love you. I really, really do with every fiber of my being," she said tearfully. "And I'm sorry. We will become everything we need to be together. I'll figure it out."

When Catherine asked God for forgiveness, she put two lives in His hands. It was questionable if the ancestors began to forgive her, too. One thing was not up for debate—she'd given up a lifestyle that was all she had known for the sake of a child who had been enslaved and sold to rotten people. She planned to move away from Alabama. She knew she had to consult with her sister about where she could go after the emancipation. It would have to be a liberal state, unlike the place she'd always known.

20

Victory and Defeat

❦⟫⟫⟫⟪⟪⟪❦

Catherine couldn't find Sarah Ann because she was away from home, doing impactful work that freed Black people appreciated. She was a committed abolitionist who remained optimistic that slavery would end across the United States. Sarah Ann felt glad that she had chosen a simpler life to contribute financially to anti-slavery societies and support the cause of abolition. She used her wealth for the sake of freedom. She stopped buying products produced by enslaved laborers. Victory had come.

"The troops have finally come to tell enslaved people that slavery exists no more! I'm exhausted from traveling around the United States, but this is what we've worked so hard for. We are one human race full of different colors," Sarah Ann said cheerfully on June 19, 1865, in Galveston, Texas.

Because Texas was the last Confederate state to inform them, enslaved Negroes in Texas didn't know they were free after the Civil War ended and the Union won. Sarah Ann clasped her hands as tears dripped from her eyes, knowing that the work of many abolitionists had helped to make the final goal possible. Major General Gordon Granger delivered the announcement known as Order No. 3 at the Osterman Building.

So much had happened two and a half years after President Lincoln issued the Emancipation Proclamation on January 1, 1863. It did not apply to all states but only to those that seceded from the United States. Delaware, Maryland, Kentucky, Missouri, and the new state of West Virginia had not been included. On top of it all, Confederate General Robert E. Lee surrendered to Union General Ulysses S. Grant at Appomattox Court House in Virginia on April 9, 1865, marking the symbolic end of the bloody Civil War. Then, on April 14, 1865, John Wilkes Booth, a Confederate supporter and successful actor, shot President Lincoln in the head while he watched a play at Ford's Theater.

Sarah Ann met two well-known abolitionists, Sarah and Angelina Grimke, the day before. Critics of slavery, they, too, had faced ridicule; they had been raised in a wealthy slaveholding family and had converted to Quakerism. When Sarah Ann found out that their brother, Henry, and an enslaved woman had a child together, she thought of Isaiah, Catherine, and Juniper. She second-guessed the advice she had given to Catherine.

"Our father owned more enslaved people than I care to admit. I'm here because my nephews, John, Archibald, and Francis, were born to Nancy Weston. We did not know that we had Negro family members at first. After we found out about their existence in an antislavery newspaper, we supported them and this movement. They are making both races proud in the academic world," Angelina said.

"Archie co-founded the NAACP. Frank studied at Princeton Theological Seminary."

"You look exhausted," Sarah Grimke said.

Sarah Ann nodded. "I am."

"You should rest. Go home," Angelina suggested.

Sarah Ann shook her head and sighed. "I can't fix generational issues in my own family if I act like this work is done without continuing to improve myself. Every problem has a root. My family has been a part of an oppressive problem. Negroes will need employment; they have no power to hire or fire."

"All of this is true," Angelina agreed, "but you can't do your best work if you run without replenishing yourself. I hope that you listen and take some time to recharge. The Freedmen's Bureau will be issuing rations and clothing, among other things."

"How do we know freed Negroes will be given the land that has been abandoned by Whites like they're supposed to receive?"

"Sarah Ann, we have been at this a long time. This process is not perfect. We work together." Angelina looked at her. "Have you seen the rest of your family?"

"Not in a while."

Sarah Grimke nodded. "Someone could be looking for you, especially if you've been missing during these chaotic times."

"That is true." Sarah Ann hadn't checked in with Catherine but needed to make the time to do so. She wondered what was going on at Rutherford Rocks. It was time to find out.

⋙⋘

The natural light faded when the sun set in Alabama. Sarah Ann sat in a comfortable plush chair. She dozed off, feeling content that slave owners could never again chain enslaved workers to the whipping post and brutalize them. The fireplace lit up her face, creating a soft glow on her skin.

Catherine entered the parlor, happy to see her sister.

"I knew you'd be back soon. I hope you don't mind that I let myself in."

Sarah Ann rubbed her tired eyes as Catherine ran to Sarah Ann, who stood. The sisters hugged and cried.

"I was wrong, Sarah Ann. I'm sorry and I need you. We're sisters. Nothing should ever ruin our relationship."

"I'm sorry, too. I need you, but I had to help the most vulnerable who have been treated harshly. God called me to change my heart."

Catherine released her sister. "I know that took a lot of courage. I admire you."

"Do you really mean that?"

"Of course I do. I suppose my economic motivation clouded my eyes. I feel so ashamed."

Slavery in America hadn't only damaged familial relationships among enslaved families; it also forced a moral wedge between relatives who owned people they never should have.

Isaiah stood quietly watching. "I found him," Catherine told Sarah Ann.

Sarah Ann bent down and ran to embrace her nephew. "You're such a beautiful little boy."

Since Isaiah looked Negro, he wouldn't have to pick a side in the community, but Sarah Ann knew that he would still face societal rejection. She decided to discuss the story her sister would tell him about who he was. For the time being, she was glad to know that he was safe and reunited with two family members. She wanted to help him regain that lost bond, but it would take time and lots of love.

Sarah Ann released Isaiah. He wasn't sure why he had come to Rutherford Rocks. He wasn't a talker who asked questions, and he was taught to take orders and listen, never to question anything.

"Rhodie has been looking for you," Sarah Ann told Catherine.

"Ah. Rhodie!" Catherine smacked her forehead.

"Could you get her? I need to have a talk with Rhodie."

"What I meant was she's gone."

"Gone?"

"I talked to everyone who decided to stay. From what I understand, she thought you'd left for good. Rhodie left with a freed couple."

"I didn't get to say goodbye. I was so fond of Rhodie. She's such a sweet and kind child. I learned a lot from her."

About half of the freed Negroes left in search of work in the North. The others accepted Mary's offer and became sharecroppers, farming the land. The only real benefit was that entire families worked together. While some began building new lives, many never stopped searching for their loved ones. They placed ads in newspapers, clinging to hope that they might one day reunite with lost family members.

Mary permitted Catherine and Isaiah to return to Rutherford Rocks. She agreed to let Catherine return to the house to gather items, arrange a move, and say farewell to whomever she liked. When they arrived, the place was half-empty because Mary had already made her demands, only allowing those who wanted to become sharecroppers to stay.

"This is a mess," Catherine admitted.

"But Aunt Sarah's children—they're here."

"That's good. I wonder where they'll go."

"About that," Sarah Ann paused. "Don't you think they should be with their mother? Just as you've reunited with— well, I won't say. I don't know what he knows yet."

"Thank you for giving me time. I haven't had time to have a talk," Catherine admitted, using her eyes.

"So, I was thinking I could help do one more thing."

"Like what?"

"Take Bessie, Wiley, and Polly to reunite with their mother."

"That's impossible. Aunt Sarah never came back to Rutherford Rocks."

"She never returned, but I do know where she is."

"How is that so? We believe she ran away."

"This would be a good time for Isaiah to have a treat."

"He's full of treats."

"More cake!" he said, smiling.

"No more." Catherine gently smiled back. "Not this time."

"How about giving him something else to do? I need to speak with you privately."

"I'll put him to bed upstairs," Catherine said, holding her son's hand.

Catherine tucked Isaiah inside her most private space. The comfort of a feather bed and linen sheets made his eyes heavy. Isaiah enjoyed proper sleep for the first time in his life. Catherine stroked his hair. She wished she could've stayed in the room to enjoy a tender part of motherhood that she missed because her son had to leave her arms.

Since Sarah Ann was patiently waiting for her sister to continue their conversation, Catherine returned to the main parlor. Sarah Ann didn't feel prepared to have an unavoidable and uncomfortable conversation, but she had no choice.

Sarah Ann's heart pounded as she told her sister parts of a story she had planned to keep a secret.

"Remember we were outside the day I admonished you for being brutal to the little boy out in the fields?"

"I do."

"You joked that I sounded like an abolitionist. Well, that's what I've been."

"*What? You?*"

"And I'm connected to more of us in Texas, not just the Underground Railroad. I helped Aunt Sarah unite with her son in Mexico. That's where he went. That's where she is. Don't be mad. I had to do it." Sarah Ann inhaled and exhaled to slow her breaths. "One more thing."

"There couldn't be more!" Catherine clutched her chest.

"I talked Aunt Sarah's children into coming with me to unite them with their mother. It would be my biggest mission as an abolitionist. I want to see their family made whole again."

A silent pause filled the air. Catherine found a chair. She felt as if the wind had been knocked out of her stomach. "This news is too much. All this time, my own sister deceived me. Aunt Sarah left although I thought she loved me. You helped her to escape right under my nose. How untrustworthy and disloyal can my own sister be to me?"

"She loved herself and her son more. You should understand that now. You were so cruel to her. She needed to be with Warren, and he needed to be with her."

Sarah Ann touched her sister's shoulder to comfort her, but she pulled away—the way used to when she got angry as a child. Sarah Ann felt their distance between them grow again.

"That's not how you're supposed to do things. Now, I don't trust you either. I have no one. I was going to ask where I should take Isaiah to live since we need to move. How could you do this to me?"

"Calm down and be reasonable, Catherine. Think beyond yourself."

"If she hadn't run away, I wouldn't have fired the overseer. Then, I wouldn't have brought Juniper here. He would still be alive. My life wouldn't be so complicated. I'm confused! You caused this disaster. I hate you!" Catherine threw a photograph of the two of them across the room.

"You're hysterical. Settle down. You'll wake Isaiah."

"Get out!" Catherine screamed at the top of her lungs.

Sarah Ann slowly shook her head. "You can't be serious. We just made up. You're going to need my help."

"I meant what I said. You took my property. Aunt Sarah was property meant to labor at Rutherford Rocks until I said she was finished! Her children should not be going to Mexico. I don't agree with this at all!"

When Catherine's last word was spoken, the sound of thunder and a bolt of thunder struck the house. Fire lit the double doors in less than thirty seconds. Thick black smoke began filling the room.

"Fire!" Catherine shouted.

As the blaze spread, a cloud of thick smoke coated the air. Catherine knocked over a candle that was housed in a portable stand, increasing the fire's strength. She stumbled while holding her breath, trying to find a bucket of water. Since enslaved workers were not around to maintain household duties, she couldn't find one. She panicked when she remembered her son was sleeping.

"Run!" Sarah Ann said, coughing.

"I can't! I have to get Isaiah. He's upstairs sleeping."

Catherine panicked when she couldn't fight the flames while stepping forward. She started coughing hard and fell to her knees. She crawled up the steps.

"Isaiah!" she screamed, shielding her face from the flames.

"You'll never make it," Sarah Ann said, pulling her back toward the door. "Run! This is our last chance!"

"Answer, Isaiah. Can you hear me?" Catherine shouted in between coughing spells.

"Run outside and tell him to jump. Let's go!"

When they made it outside, they could see Isaiah crying through an upstairs window. Although the fire remained confined to the first floor, he refused to jump.

"Jump for Mommy! Jump!" Catherine screamed, motioning for him to push the window up and jump.

Isaiah, a fearful little boy, was too submissive to take a chance of jumping alone. He dropped from view and curled into a ball on the floor.

When Catherine couldn't see his face, she lost control and headed back inside the Great House.

"No!" Sarah Ann screamed. "Don't."

Catherine bolted forward through the flames. Sarah Ann ran toward the edge of the yard to remove herself from the heat of the flames.

The massive explosion rocked Rutherford Rocks. Freed Negroes came running toward the Great House. Aunt Sarah's children stood behind Sarah Ann as the flames touched the sky. Sarah Ann fell on the grass and cried. She knew Catherine and Isaiah were dead.

21

Not the Same as It Ever Was

"The structure of such a beautiful home is gone. The columns are the only things left," Mary said, ogling the Great House upon visiting Rutherford Rocks. She knew the property could be gutted and cleared, but Mary felt that the freed Negroes would pretend to be victimized if she tried to profit from rehabbing it.

"They would be harder to control and harder to satisfy while engaging in hard labor. It ain't worth it," Mary complained to her husband, Tom.

Mary tried to help Catherine after Isaiah was born. She warned her not to become attached, but Catherine wouldn't let go of the emotional bond and had lost control.

Mary thought of their conversation and shook her head at the choices the deceased woman had made.

"Do you even care that a boy and someone you know died in the fire, my dear?" Tom asked.

Mary shrugged. "Not really. This is a good mess to avoid. I don't want this cursed property. I have another potential property for sharecroppers."

Mary's mind was on lucrative real estate investments, not on being kinder. She smelled the charred ruins at Rutherford Rocks while sipping on a glass of red wine.

"I'm very happy that I hadn't delivered the money for the sale. That's something big to celebrate."

"Do you ever think of more than money?"

"Not really. Money is my reward for putting up with you." She winked.

"Likewise. We're birds of a feather."

"That's why I want you to stay until I'm just bones in my grave." Mary wiggled her fingers to flash her large diamond wedding ring.

৩৩১

After Catherine's and Isaiah's burial, Sarah Ann helped freed Blacks relocate before she headed to Mexico with Bessie, Wiley, and Polly.

"My children!" Aunt Sarah said, hugging each child who longed to have her hugs and kisses countless mornings and nights.

They thought they would never see each other again.

Warren walked over to Sarah Ann, looking at her face-to-face. "You will be blessed with long life, prosperity, and future happiness. What you've done for my family has no price, no value I could ever assess. I don't know why you picked us out of all the people you could've helped. You risked your life to reunite a mother with her family, not once, but twice."

Tears dripped from Warren's eyes—a man who had never cried, but Sarah Ann's insistence on being generous, kind, and choosing what was right over color and race moved him to show unfettered emotion.

"I pray that you never know hunger or disappointment. May you always find the love you deserve, and may your family be blessed."

Aunt Sarah turned around. She looked toward the heavens, asking God to lift the curse that she had placed on Catherine's womb and life in those pearly gates.

Aunt Sarah smiled. "No one can tell me that angels don't exist. Whenever I die, I can say I know how to read and speak better because of you. I found happiness with my son. I will take these years and cherish them. I thank you for everything that you did, both spoken and unspoken. I can see the pain in your eyes. I don't know the things that happened after I left Rutherford Rocks, but I reckon I will find out. I have a real chance to be free. I know I'm one of the lucky ones."

Sarah Ann couldn't hold back the tears that she shed in honor of equality and freedom. The loss of two family members saddened her, but unknowingly, Aunt Sarah's prayers and sincere repentance covered her with grace. Catherine had to pay for Juniper's loss of life. The debt was too great for God to spare her or the product of a heinous act.

Many lost their lives at Rutherford Rocks plantation—innocent men lynched, commonplace abuse—but it also highlighted a story of survival. Tragic events prevented Mary Rector from turning the land into a place where sharecropping would make economic slaves out of freed Negroes who needed a fresh start. The tainted land became a symbolic representation of joy and pain, resilience and new life—the rebirth of a better tomorrow for enslaved people who made it out alive. No one would benefit from a place where evil tore lives apart. And that's when the curse at Rutherford Rocks broke like an open sea. Labor would never be free or cheap again. The barren land told a story along with a historical marker that shared just a mere piece of Rutherford Rocks' history.

22

A Little Too Late

The sun hung high and heavy, dragging its heat down on their backs like a hot skillet left too long on the stove. Dry, red dirt clung to their ankles and got in their shoes, thick as flour, sticking between their toes. Pine trees stood off on either side of the road, tall and lean, whispering nothing useful in the breeze. Here and there, blackbirds stirred up dust, flapping low over scattered cow patties and wooden fence posts, leaning like tired men.

Hazel and her offspring—Rosalind and Bradley—walked a narrow path, just wide enough for a mule cart, but there were no wheels behind them now—just tired feet, slow steps, and long shadows.

Rosalind yelped. "Slow down, Bradley! I tripped on a rock and almost twisted my ankle."

Bradley kept ahead, shoulders back, his silhouette sharp against the glare. "Settle your nerves and tighten up your attitude," he replied, barely slowing.

"My brother is supposed to look out for me."

"If Momma is older than us and she can keep up on this long, dirt road, I don't see why your legs won't carry you to and fro. You've been complaining about walkin' the whole trip. Walk, gal!"

They passed a crooked gate where two goats peeked through the gaps, chewing like they had all the time in the world. A dog barked once from some far-off yard and then fell quiet again. No wagons. No people. Just air thick with dust and heat.

Rosalind's knees bent before she collapsed. "Your words could be far sweeter. I can't adjust feet that never done this much walking in life just 'cause we been set free as the wind."

The road curved slightly to the left, revealing more of the same—stubborn ground, scattered brush, and fence lines sagging like old bones. Insects buzzed in the stillness, slicing the quiet in short, sharp notes.

Bradley looked back over his shoulder. "Summon your will to leave Rutherford Rocks and stop openin' your mind ta let go. The reason why we have to go someplace else in Alabama is because Whites owning Negroes has ended. If that don't make ambition stick around in yo' mind, nothing will ever get you to move out of this dirt. That red color is gonna make you filthy."

A rusty cowbell clanked from somewhere off in a pasture, maybe a half-mile back, the sound drifting like it didn't care who heard it.

"I need some time to get myself together whether I'm in pursuit of freedom or not." Rosalind flexed her feet. "I can't take one more step. I'm beat."

They passed a fence where vines strangled the boards, green fingers wrapped around splintered wood. No houses close enough to beg from, and no sign of water except the dry ditch running alongside the road.

"Life don't give nuthin' good for certain to Negroes like us. You sound like Missus used ta when she was complainin' about everything."

Hazel stopped in her tracks. "I know you trying to help, Bradley, but we have been walking for at least an hour and a half. Maybe it's time for us to take a break from dis walking. We not mules. Ain't no peace of mind of pushin' the body dis' way. In slavery, there wasn't no room to complain. Freedom tastes a whole lot different."

She looked out ahead, blinking through perspiration. Her dress clung to her back, soaked from the heat and the worry. The sun glared down without mercy, turning even the shade into a warm breath on the neck.

"There's no place to go, and Rosalind is making the trip longer."

"You're not in charge of me—when I walk or where I rest," Rosalind spewed. "You've got one more time to throw disrespect in my ear."

Now, in disgust, Hazel shook her head. "This ain't no time to turn on each other. We're all we've got. We left one world behind, and the time come to move on to another. Now walkin' a long way is a sacrifice, but we gotta get determined to find a place where we belong. You two take a deep breath and put the bickering behind you. We can neva stop lovin' each other. People who ran out of love and respect is the reason why slavery started in the first place."

Bradley adjusted his tone. "Yes, ma'am."

"Help your sister up."

Bradley bent down to lend a hand to Rosalind. She stood to her feet.

"I'm sorry, everyone. I'll try again. I don't want us losing lots of time on account of me."

Hazel smiled at her daughter. "That's da spirit. Good girl."

Rosalind, Bradley, and Hazel wiped the sweat from their brows, their destination still unknown. Hazel's eyes were bloodshot. She wanted to close them and rest from all the noise in her head but didn't. Couldn't. She just squared her shoulders, like somebody pretending not to cry in church, and told herself to keep strong—for them.

The air smelled of dry grass and something sour—maybe the ghost of something once dead in the trees.

For the first time in too long, she prayed to God for understanding. Something inside her felt like it had broken loose and needed fixing. She hadn't been above nor below no one at Rutherford Rocks, but still, she'd let Massa Brower treat her like she was different. Better. It didn't make her life easier. It made her heart quieter. That was worse.

Hazel pushed herself to keep her eyes open and encouraged Rosalind to walk another half a mile.

"Good news. I think I sees a church this way," Hazel pointed out, "down the road. Goin' dere might save a lot of worry."

"I'll try to make it, but I can't promise that I can. At least someone could've given us a wagon ride when slaves were freed," Rosalind whined. "I'm so thirsty, I'd be willing to drink cold water from a dirty river."

Bradley smirked at his sister. "Shut your mouth! We got it."

"Look." Rosalind pointed. "Maybe we can stop over there."

"Gal, it might not be safe," Hazel said.

"We can say we're looking for sharecropping work if it's not," Rosalind retorted.

Rosalind had the freedom to take more chances because of her very light complexion. She feared less, even in times when she should've feared more. The girl smoothed her wet hair that had gotten drenched in the rain. Bradley and Hazel were also wet from the torrential downpour. Hazel struggled to hold on to her ability to walk until she felt it was safe enough to stop. Rosalind behaved as if she was the queen of the world, having the courage to wander off the path to a long entrance that was lined with bushes and a white picket fence.

"You never listen. Don't go," Bradley cautioned.

Rosalind rolled her eyes and pushed her beautiful brown curls away from her face. She ignored Bradley's advice, even though he was the only male. Her defiance led both Bradley and Hazel to follow her. Hazel tried to feel less anxious when she saw beautiful flowers and rose bushes. She had always loved them. The two-story house was large and rustic, with land surrounding it as far as the eye could see. Hazel assumed that a White family lived there.

"A missus must feel lucky to live in a fancy house like this," Hazel said.

Rosalind tapped on the door with great urgency.

When it opened, Hazel's heart raced as her daughter began to ask if it would be okay to rest there for just a little while.

"I don't see why not. Others have stopped on the way out of Alabama," the man said.

He was the color of the darkest onyx. Rosalind couldn't speak at first, so she just smiled and waved.

"It's okay. Come on," the man told Hazel and Bradley.

The man, who had just collected tomatoes in his garden, opened the door wider. He took a closer look at Rosalind. "I've seen you someplace before."

"Are you sure?" She tilted her head.

"I'm certain of it."

"That's right. You're the one who stopped by Rutherford Rocks to see my mother."

Henry nodded. "Correct."

Hazel and Bradley walked up to the front steps. "Henry?" A lump grew in her throat. She felt vulnerable, sorry that she hadn't accepted his offer of marriage.

"Is something wrong, Momma?" Bradley asked.

"I need to sit down. Dat's all." Hazel lowered her body to sit on the porch steps.

"He offered for us to come in. Why sit there?" Rosalind asked.

Hazel didn't think she'd see Henry again for a thousand years. She felt in her gut that Henry owned the beautiful home and property where they'd stopped. He had tried to tell her all about it at Rutherford Rocks, but she had been condescending, doubtful, and turned down the possibility of marriage.

Henry bent down, looking Hazel in the eyes with compassion. The obstacle of rejection hadn't burdened him since Hazel made it clear that she'd abandoned her love for him. He looked like he was aging backward and had even gotten his chipped teeth fixed. This small cosmetic improvement made him devastatingly handsome. Hazel noticed both small and great things that made Henry who he was physically. She was overtaken with an overflow of positive energy and manliness. He still had the heart of a great man. This time, he was in a position to show his generosity.

"If you want to come in, have something to eat, and get dry, you and your children can do that."

Hazel couldn't believe he still offered. Bradley helped his mother up as Rosalind eagerly accepted Henry's invitation. Henry joined Bradley in pulling Hazel to her feet.

The three visitors were happy to come inside when the rain resumed. Henry gave them towels to dry themselves and changes of clothes.

"We'll give them back," Hazel said.

"Relax. It's okay. Have some tea. I'll get something to eat."

"I told Momma not to be so doubtful and scared," Rosalind said.

"Your momma is right to be cautious. Not everyone likes free Negroes, and the Negro Codes will make it hard to get ahead. I hear that Mississippi and South Carolina will be the first to pass them. Negroes are gonna be required to have written proof of having a job every year. Wages will be low, or Negro people can be arrested if the rules aren't followed. Anyone who doesn't farm or work as a servant is gonna have to pay taxes, too. There's more to it. I don't recommend heading to either of those states."

"That doesn't sound like freedom to me." Rosalind sipped tea.

"Maybe we can stay here in Alabama, I mean," Hazel said.

Bradley touched his sister's arm. "Let's see if it's still raining."

"But I'm not finished with my tea."

Henry told Bradley and Rosalind that it would be okay to rest in the back room until dinner was ready. Rosalind took a final swallow of tea, catching her brother's hint.

When they left, she cracked the door to listen to her mother and Henry talk.

"Grown folks' conversation is none of your business," Bradley told his sister.

"You act like a serious old man. Lighten up, Brad."

Bradley shut the door. "You go too far. Rest until we're called."

"Thank you for letting us stop here," Hazel said.

"I've done it for others."

"You have a really nice place."

"I think so. It's home. Thank you."

Hazel suddenly realized that Henry had power, money, determination, and traits of resilience. He was a visual depiction of a pharaoh who should be held in high regard. He looked more handsome than he had in his younger years. Hazel recalled their time laughing in the sun. Henry looked well-rested after he'd stopped to enjoy his finished home. Hazel stood like she wanted to tell him something.

"I've missed you very much," she said.

"I don't think I heard you right."

"You did." She moved closer to kiss him.

Henry backed away. "I just want to help because your girl knocked on this door for help. You said to never come looking for you again. I honored your wishes and didn't."

"I made a mistake and regret what I said. You're right; my boy's gonna need a man to teach him about the world. I wanted to be with you for a long time. This is the perfect place for the four of us to be."

She finally realized the value of her children being raised in a two-parent household. Her only chances to parent had been unpleasant and burdensome. Hazel had seen at least half of the women she knew raising their little ones alone because fathers had been sent away. Henry could provide a family structure that no master could tear apart.

With these thoughts in mind, Hazel walked toward Henry again. His back touched a wall. She pressed her lips against his. "Now that slavery is over, let me make it up to you. I want to get married now."

Henry gently pushed her away, filled with doubt. "You told me things had changed. I adjusted to the changes you pointed out. You guided me to see the truth when you treated me like a worthless coward."

"What's that supposed to mean?"

"You ruined my plan by not following what I wanted to start. This is the end for you and me."

He didn't want a woman who only wanted to benefit from his hard work. Hazel had doubted his capabilities and his offer of stability and love. Henry felt that freedom would come, somehow. Even if he had to pay for his woman's freedom, he was willing to invest in her future.

"Foolishness. You love me, and I've got two good kids who are gonna love you back." Hazel unbuttoned the top of the dress she had borrowed.

"Have you ever stopped to think whose clothes you're using?"

"Yours." She continued to unbutton her dress.

A woman emerged from the kitchen. "Or maybe it's mine. I'm Cecilia."

Hazel jumped. She scrambled to fix the dress. Henry had closed his heart and buried the thought of loving Hazel like a pile of bones. Another woman who was fond of Henry had replaced Hazel.

"The pleasure is all mine. I'm his wife." Cecilia held out her hand.

Hazel didn't know whether to laugh or cry. She felt like a buzzard picking through someone else's leftovers. Cecilia was warm, sweet, and easygoing. She trusted her husband and wasn't jealous of what Hazel tried to do. Henry had told her about a woman he once loved. She guessed that somehow, Hazel had come back for closure during freedom.

"I didn't know," Hazel said apologetically.

She angrily turned to Henry. "I don't want to slow you down. I'll be getting out of the way. Bradley! Rosalind! We got to go!"

Hazel's children scuffled to the living room, wondering what was wrong. "I thought we were staying for dinner," Rosalind said.

"Miss Cecilia might not like that. Henry didn't ask his *wife*."

"I don't mind. All of you are more than welcome to stay," Cecilia said.

Hazel felt like gouging Cecilia's eyes out because she suddenly valued Henry and could not have him back. She hunted for her wet clothes, feeling bitter and regretful. Hazel changed clothes in the back room, feeling her still-drenched dress cling to her skin. Jealousy drove her to toss Cecilia's dress at Henry.

"Cecilia won't love you like I do. We're gonna always love each other, no matter what, just the way you said when we were young at Rutherford Rocks. If you didn't have these nice things, she wouldn't be here with you."

Hazel started to tell Cecilia that if she really wanted to return and take Henry, she could do it. Massa Brower taught her that sharing a married man wasn't off limits.

Instead, Hazel looked at Cecilia. "I suppose you was in the right place at the right time. Treat him good, or I will."

Cecilia frowned at the mixed message that she didn't completely understand.

"Respect my lady, Hazel. We opened our home to you and your children."

He wanted to remind Hazel that she was the one who allowed Massa Brower to break their bond, but he skipped speaking the truth.

"We'll see how long it takes before you get sick of Ms. Cecilia," Hazel swiftly responded.

"This home is blessed, and it's gonna stay that way. A jealous woman needs to get her own man," Cecilia retorted.

"I'm not jealous; I'm regretful. There's a big difference."

"Henry is married now. You had your chance and should really learn to be happy for others. Since you can't, you should be fixin' to leave now."

"The man of the house should be the one telling me to go, but before that happens, I'll leave on my own. I love you, Henry. I know that you'll always love me back." Hazel winked.

Cecilia crossed her arms defensively. She knew that Hazel had spent too much time doubting Henry. When he looked lonely, she settled his fears. When the garden needed weeding, she bent over and helped him out. She made him laugh under the stars and rubbed his back when it ached from fixing up the house. She was never loud or mean. When Hazel turned down Henry's marriage proposal, Cecilia remembered to build him back up, encouraging him to shed the insecurities Hazel had planted.

"She and I were close," Henry had once said.

"I'm sorry she did that to you," Cecilia replied.

She told Henry he was a good man while pressing his head against her ample bosom, letting her plump body warm his flesh. She didn't have to be the prettiest, smartest, or the best; she just needed to be there for a man who had done more than most White or Negro men in profiting from slavery.

Henry still loved Hazel, and Cecilia could sense the truth. It was hard for him to watch a woman he loved struggling on her own with two children depending on her, but Hazel had damaged his belief in true love. Since Henry had been more than fair to Hazel, he decided that he'd learn to love Cecilia as much as he could.

"Be safe," Henry said.

He wanted to tell Hazel that he loved her, too, but he couldn't. Bradley turned around and Henry waved at the boy who could've been a son to him. Bradley wished that a man like Henry had been his pappy, even if it wasn't by blood. Massa Brower had been an absent father who impregnated his mother by force. He had damaged his identity, never caring to know him as a human being. But Henry wanted to know his favorite colors, understand what he could do to help rebuild a damaged boy and be a father to a boy who never had an active father, physically or emotionally.

Henry restrained himself from releasing tears from his eyes. He wanted to break the cycle of fatherless Negro boys to be a better example for Bradley. He usually wasn't given much attention. Bradley was soft-spoken and gentle, never wanting to make a scene wherever he went. No one poured into his life as a boy. Bradley was a former child of the plantation who had no hopes and dreams of his own. He felt connected to Henry, even though they had never had a conversation. Henry released the idea of fatherhood when he could hold their gaze no longer.

"Goodbye, Bradley," he said, wishing he could take him under his wing as a son.

This time, Cecilia joined hands with Henry as they watched Hazel, Rosalind, and Bradley disappear down the road.

Hazel regained her strength to leave the only man who ever truly loved her. Unfortunately, her realization was a little too late.

23

An Unexpected Gift

❀>>><<<❀

The burdens of newfound freedom weighed on Hazel and the two children who depended on her to determine their future path.

"Nothin' too great to lose hope. We're in His loving care," Hazel reminded, trying to restore her children's broken spirits.

Hazel had no idea how she would feed her two hungry children by morning, with no food and no resources to sustain them. She inhaled as memories of Massa Brower flooded her mind—his hat in her hand, leaning in to kiss her. She recalled with bitter clarity the day he sent Henry away. Though jittery and angry, she had forced herself to accept his advances, fearing the lash if she refused.

The sight of Henry being married to another woman had sparked Hazel's temper. She stopped walking as tears flowed.

"What's wrong, Momma?" Bradley asked.

"Nothing," Hazel lied, plopping on a fallen log.

She couldn't bear to tell her son that she was heartsick over slavery's twisted legacy—a system that had turned Henry into a rebellious success while leaving her adrift. Regret had become her private prison. How she wished she hadn't doubted Henry's potential.

"We have a long way to go, Momma. If you don't get going, Rosalind will forget how to use her legs."

"I need a little rest this time, son. I got a lot on my heart."

Rosalind bent down and placed her arms around her mother. "I know I can be a lot to deal with. I'll try to do better."

"It's not you. Sometimes, being strong falls off de bones. I's tired and feeling a little weak."

"Rosalind being nice is no small victory, Momma. You better let the gal rest from her tricks."

"What we're going through is my fault."

"What do you mean?" Rosalind asked.

"I was too loyal to the wrong person, and not loyal enough to the right one. That's why we're in this position."

Bradley and Rosalind comforted their mother, massaging her back.

"You was a slave, Momma. Our pappy made you serve him and have us. I saw the way you looked at Mr. Henry. You loved him, but you were stopped from giving him your heart when you wanted to," Bradley said.

"How did you know all that? What makes you think you have what's on Momma's mind? Our pappy wasn't a bad man. He loved us," Rosalind snapped.

"Your brother does have a lot more figured out than I knew how to explain to you two."

"But Pappy was not bad. He loved us," Rosalind insisted.

"This a complicated conversation, Rosalind. Your pappy owned us and before you were born, he sold Henry to separate him from me."

"You're not telling the truth." Tears started filling Rosalind's eyes. "He loved me."

Hazel looked up at her daughter. "I's sorry. I never meant to talk about this, but what I said was the truth."

Bradley pouted. "Our pappy was not a good man. You read all those books about slavery. I'm certain you figured dat out."

Rosalind folded her arms over her chest. "He let me play with dolls. He let me eat good food. And I look like him. Are you telling me that I'm a bad person?"

"That sick man broke me and he broke my dreams. I didn't want no kids wit' him. I was made to do it until bending his way got easier. He drove Missus crazy, and she was 'sposed to be one of them moral-minded Christian church folk from a wealthy family. Yassuh, they both dead anyway. Those are the cold, hard facts of life wit' Massa Brower," Hazel screamed.

Rosalind struggled to find the right words. "You don't love me."

"That's not what I said. You and dis' boy is all I got. Don't matter now how you got here. "

Bradley touched his sister's shoulder. "Momma's in a lot of pain. She didn't say nothin' that harsh. Don't go puttin' lyin' words in her mouth."

Rosalind covered her face as tears leaked through her fingers. "It's easy for you to say. You don't look like our massa."

"You and me are here now," Bradley said. "Love is shown by the way people treat you year after year. Momma been treatin' us good our whole lives. You can't deny that, can you?"

"You're right about that, Brad."

"Then Momma is our hero, not Massa Brower, even if he was our pappy."

Hazel wiped tears from her eyes. "I'm feelin' better now. Let's get back to walkin'."

They had comforted each other as best they could. The trio fell silent when they saw a horse and wagon round the corner and come to a halt.

"Woah," Cecilia said, stopping the horse. She stepped down from the wagon. "I was looking for the three of you."

"Why? Is everything okay?" Hazel asked.

"I had a talk with Henry about you not having any place to go with Bradley and Rosalind. Our home has been a stop as a safe house on the Underground Railroad before slavery ended. If we've helped strangers, I see no reason why we can't help you."

"Are you saying we can come back?" Rosalind asked.

Cecilia turned to Hazel. "This isn't an offer to live with us full time, forever, but come back and work on a plan at our place if ya want to."

"We want to! I'm so relieved." Rosalind headed toward the wagon, then stopped.

"Not so fast, Cecilia. Is dis' some kind of tricka?" Hazel asked.

"Let me clear up one thing first. I failed to separate participation in the movement from my personal feelings about you and my husband's past. Your children are innocent in all of this. Being born was not their choice, but making a better life should be. We want them to know their own potential. It would be a shame for them to lose everything, including self-respect. That's the only reason I came to offer temporary support. Me and Henry know you have nowhere to take them. If you don't want no help, I won't come back. I was washing clothes and stopped what I was doing to try to find you three to extend this offer."

After Hazel and her two children had left, Cecilia had grown restless and spoke to Henry about a nagging feeling.

"Henry, I got something to say about what just happened."

"Speak on it."

"How can emancipation help former slaves and their children to break out of a life of servitude if they don't have no plan and no place to go? We know sharecropping's a trap for the common man and so is domestic work. They gon' keep winning and people who been set free gon' keep losing with systems like these. Young people deserve a better chance than the same thing happening. The only difference is plantation doors are closed but the business of it is still the same."

"What chu' sayin, Cecilia?"

"I been thinkin' of the way our place has been a safe house for people escaping before slavery ended, and I been tossing around that look you gave that fine boy, Bradley, like you wanted to pat him on da head. I know their momma was sassy, but I don't feel good about the way they headed down that road with nothin'. How would you feel if I asked if they wanted to come back so we can put together our thoughts and plans?"

"Community building is important, but don't be mad if the conversation don't go the way you think. Hazel is in a bad place over me."

"This not my first rodeo over two women wantin' one man."

"But couples like us couldn't legally marry until slavery ended. How many times dis' happen?"

"Hazel would be mad at me if she knew we done only legally checked that box a day ago after you straightened out my freedom."

"Only one woman can claim the prize."

"Is that what you think you are—a prize?"

Henry laughed. "I am whatever you want to call me as long as its respectful."

"As long as you can adjust to the pressure go on and look for Hazel and her children with my wagon."

Pride gnawed at Hazel's resolve, but it was Cecilia who had asked her husband to intervene and help. Hazel crossed her arms as Cecilia explained more about why she had sought them out.

"You got to challenge your expectations of a woman who married Henry. I ain't here to intimidate with trick words. I'm offerin' to unfold my arms to empower 'cause unity is that important."

"I's speechless," Hazel replied.

"How about accepting some help. No one else is offering us to step up in their wagon and go home with them," Bradley suggested.

Hazel could not deny the truth. She had no formal education, training, or emergency funds to cushion the blow of pain and loss of a broken home.

"Okay. We gon' come wit' you," she told Cecilia.

Bradley and Rosalind tried to hurry into the wagon.

"Don't forget to help your momma up first. Always respect her. That's mighty important in life," Cecilia explained.

They gave Hazel a boost before hopping inside the wagon, headed for a new beginning.

24

Old Love, New Bonds

⟨⟨⟨⟩⟩⟩

"Thank you, Mr. Henry. You saved us from sweltering heat and a dusty road leadin' someplace. Our Momma don't know where," Rosalind said, sipping a glass of lemonade.

It was December 1865. After Cecilia had parked the wagon, Henry had just finished taking the mule to pasture to graze. He walked to the house, where he greeted Hazel, Bradley, and Rosalind. They were enjoying a cool drink while sitting at the kitchen table.

"I'm glad to see all of you again. You welcome, Rosalind."

"How about slave catchers? They got them over here?" Bradley asked, his brow furrowed.

"No one owns us anymore, silly. Who they gon' return us to if they catch us on a road? They can't catch slaves any mo'," Rosalind said, wiping sweat from her brow.

"I don't trust them, and I don't trust this emancipation thing," Bradley replied.

"Freedom for everyone is true, but there's still bad people out here who wan' freed Negroes to pay for the price of Union rebellion and victory. It's not safe for a woman and chillun. That's why Miss Cecilia come lookin' for y'all wit' my wagon," Henry explained.

Hazel kept her gaze on the ground, feeling wrapped in a complex web of emotions. She felt ashamed she hadn't been more resilient. Henry and his wife had rescued another man's children from sweat-stained clothes and were walking alongside her in despair. She hated taking shelter from Henry and his kind-hearted wife. Her thoughts told the unspoken story of stubborn emotions, but Hazel hid her deep regret about rejecting Henry's love.

"I reckon I should thank you and your missus for lettin' us come back. I sorry for my behavior. Yo Cecilia is mighty kind-hearted and fine. I see why you jump da broom wit' her."

The air grew thick with tension after Hazel spoke. Henry knew that Hazel's heart ached. He wished he could absorb her embarrassment, even hold her in his arms. Cecilia's eyes searched her husband's face, looking for signs that Henry loved Hazel more than her.

Henry searched for empathetic words that would spare both women's feelings and found them.

"My Cecilia surely been a blessin' to me and a whole legion. As of today, we family. Ain't no competition behind these doors. We work together, day by day, one step at a time."

Rosalind stood in the kitchen doorway. "I'm happy to have a second chance to be safe and treated like a human bein.' Nobody who left Rutherford Rocks wanted us to join them."

"Why don't you make me a promise," Cecilia asked, giving a warm smile.

"If it's okay wit' your momma, call me Aunt Cecilia. While you're here, our home is your home. And over der is yo' Uncle Henry."

Rosalind smiled. Hazel gave a permissive nod.

"Let's make use of that kitchen. Help me cut these potatoes and set da table for dinner. We gotta get some meat on ya bones."

"What should I do to help?" Hazel asked.

"Rest. You been out here wit' these chil'ren, walkin' and worryin'. Negro women need to take more breaks. We been taught to be gentles to a missus, but it's a new day."

"Aunt Cecilia, before we go, I have a question to ask," Rosalind said.

"What is it, chile?"

"When is that boy gon' get a haircut?"

"Ain't nobody to do it." Bradley frowned at his sister.

"Uncle Henry can, after you pull some garden weeds and sweep the walkway. He won' mind. He's good at things like that," Cecilia said.

Bradley smiled. "Really?"

"If it's okay wit' Hazel, consider dat haircut done," Henry replied.

"Can I?" Bradley asked, wide-eyed.

"Yessum, boy."

Rosalind ran out of the house after cutting potatoes and setting the table. She couldn't resist picking wildflowers to add to an empty vase on a table. Hazel's heart nearabout skipped a beat when she realized she was alone with Cecilia.

"We didn't come to kick up our heels and relax, we come to work. I got my energy up again after dat wagon ride and break," Hazel explained.

"Since you family now, I's give you a chance to earn money around the house helping with tasks. You can save while we get a plan."

"I can't take no mo' than food and shelter fo' me and my youngins."

"We not rivals. It don't take blood to be family, but it does take da right spirit."

"Sure 'nuf," Hazel agreed.

"You gon' need help for the future. Henry want everyone to be happy and takin' care of right. We'll do what we can."

"Your generosity got me having a tear in my eye."

"I'm just treatin' you the way I'd want to be treated. If you don't mind me askin', is that fine Rosalind of yours and Bradley chillun of the plantation? You know, are they from a massa?"

"You already know the answer."

"They gon' need better doses of discipline and a taste of how to make it out here as Negroes. One drop and that's what they are. I don't get the idea they use to doin' back-breakin' work or much at all."

"They gon' fit in here the short time we put down our roots at your house better than the whole time they came up at Rutherford Rocks."

Hazel was too ashamed to explain that colorism had permeated their family and rendered them helpless, empty-handed, and the butt of mean-spirited jokes. Hazel had thought that her children's light complexions would bring them a better fortune in life, but John Brower's DNA continued to cause them never-ending pain.

Rosalind interrupted the conversation when she raced back to the house with flowers, a smile, and excitement. "Aunt Cecilia, can I put these in here?" She grabbed a vase.

"Nothin' like sprucin' up a room with a child's joy. Go right ahead."

Rosalind saved one flower. "And this one's for you." She handed it to Cecilia.

Cecilia smiled and embraced the girl as Hazel watched. She'd never seen Rosalind so happy and motivated to help complete tasks and behave so thoughtfully. It took little time for Bradley or Rosalind to feel comfortable and learn to pitch in as part of a family unit.

"Look. Uncle Henry cut my hair?" Bradley said, also appearing.

"You look mighty fine now, Brad," Henry said, resting his right hand on the boy's shoulder.

"Thank you for helping me."

Henry patted the boy on the back as if he had forged a fatherly bond with Bradley. "Maybe we can go fishin' tomorrow after we do some chores, if you be interested in that."

"Really? No man ever took me fishin."

"I wouldn't want Brad to turn into some troublesome pest to you," Hazel interrupted.

"Nonsense. I wanna take him if you'll let 'em go. There's a pond over yonder."

"I spot a pile of wood on the side of the house. Can we chop some of that, too, Uncle Henry?"

Hazel took a deep breath. "It's alright wit' me."

Bradley cheered, leaving his mother feeling like she had nothing to offer.

Hazel agreed and felt left out, but it wasn't right to feel unhappy for her children, who had gained acceptance and an extended family while learning to shed their spoiled behavior.

"Not so fast. Dinner's ready," Cecilia said. "Everybody wash ya hands before we pray and eat. There's a basin of water over there."

ಌಠಡ

Days of unexpected help from Henry and his wife turned into weeks, then several months of sunrises and sunsets of living in harmony with Henry and Cecilia. Cecilia paid Hazel every week for spinning, weaving, sewing, and gardening a new patch of land. Since Cecilia had more help, she could sell fresh vegetables in the community. It didn't take long for Rosalind to enjoy having an aunt who would teach her things and give her the attention she always wanted. Since Rosalind could already read well, she was able to help with recordkeeping and mathematical work. Cecilia arranged for Rosalind and Bradley to attend a schoolhouse that was set up by the Northern Aid Society.

"You must know how to read and write," she told Bradley. "And Rosalind need ta get out of this Southern oppression mess and go to college. There ain't no use in you bein' poor."

"But I'm not smart like my sister. I doubt I'll need those skills, but yes, ma'am."

"How will you take care of yourself, read contracts, or know when someone is cheating you when you get paid in de future? Reading, writing, and learning the basics is important. School is just three hours a day. Your momma goes to learn at night. Be gentle with yourself. You'll get it."

Cecilia and Henry believed Hazel was expanding her knowledge at night, but she was worried that Cecilia would turn on her and tell Henry to toss her out with two children. No matter how kind they were, Hazel didn't trust their motives. When she met Caroline Weaver, Hazel believed that her time at night was better used working for the White woman to save a nest egg faster to get on her feet. She started feeling protective of her pride around the time she met Caroline Weaver, owner of a nearby farmstead.

"I need help making dairy products and help in the chicken houses."

"I can do the work, but I won't be available in da day much."

"I just need someone who knows what to do."

Hazel recalled her own hurtful experience with colorism while working for White women who wanted her to do it all around the house, even when they hired her to do a specific task. Hazel scrubbed clothes against a washboard in a washtub before ironing and folding piles of clean clothes. Mrs. Weaver paid Hazel the agreed amount at first. Then, she couldn't understand that when a person worked for something, they needed to be paid. She was afraid to complain about unpaid wages when she tried to charge the market rate for doing such hard work.

God heard her pleas, but the employer wanted cheap labor. Mrs. Weaver's moral views remained unchanged. She did not feel that Hazel and Rosalind deserved a fair working wage.

"If I don't get my money, I'll get put out of where we stay," Hazel lied.

"Sign a contract. I'll pay you in food and clothes but not money. Work for me for two years."

"I can't read, and I'm not signing no paper. Lately, you been getting me to do washerwoman work and cooking. We neva talked about that."

"You needed work, and I gave it to you. Now you want me to sing your praises for an easy job anyone could do."

"Then do it yourself! I quit!"

"You're making a terrible mistake," Mrs. Weaver shouted, her hands placed on her hips.

"I won't bow my head. Should I get the law involved, or should you?"

"I'll scream or do whatever I want in my home."

"Not when slavery is over."

Mrs. Weaver slapped Hazel, forcing her to remember her days of battling with Catherine at Rutherford Rocks. Hazel returned the favor, slapping Mrs. Weaver silly.

"You savage! How dare you? I'm gettin' the sheriff on you!"

A sense of panic surged through Hazel as she recalled her run-ins with Catherine. She bolted from Mrs. Weaver's property, hoping for emotional rest and financial favor to flow like a river some place absent of injustice and discrimination. The run-in with Mrs. Weaver led Hazel to panic, shake her children to awaken them in bed, and demand that they dress to leave.

A sleepy Rosalind rubbed her eyes with her knuckles. "What's going on?"

"It's time ta get on the road. Gather your things. There's been some trouble. We gots ta leave."

"Why?"

"Don't' ask just lissen. Wake your brother."

Hazel scurried to gather items around the room.

"I don't want to leave Aunt Cecilia. I like her," Rosalind whined.

"I must answer for my deeds on my own. We done worn out our welcome here. The help has been a blessing. Write a note," Hazel demanded.

Rosalind cried as she searched in another room for a quill pen made of goose feathers, ink, and paper after telling her brother they had to leave.

"No! I don't want to leave Uncle Henry. He changed my life," the boy hollered.

"Our momma said so. Get ready."

Hazel walked into the room. "Stayin' here was temporary, anyway. It's time to go."

Henry wiped the sleep from his eyes. "Now? Why? I ain't goin'!"

Hazel's voice escalated. "You used ta lissen to everything I said. Now you grown sassy, and yo sister the one who lissen."

The disturbance awakened Henry and Cecilia, causing them to rush from their bedroom to the commotion.

"What's the meaning of this?" Henry asked.

"Our momma tryin' to make us leave in the middle of the night," Bradley complained.

"Hazel—what's wrong wit' you, treatin' these chilluns like puppets? Let 'em rest."

"Since you must know, I was doin' a little work for a Missus Weaver. I had some trouble outta her and slapped her. She try to make me get into a contract and wouldn't pay me right for the work I done."

Cecilia stood by Henry's side. "I been payin' you—me and Henry. We know there's still a racial divide that should be carefully navigated. Some people still real upset slavery is over."

Henry added, "Why would you turn to Mrs. Weaver? We know her all right. She got Negroes sharecropping and rippin' 'em off around here. They don' signed their lives away. She neva had to take care of nothin' herself until slavery ended."

"I didn't know she was like dat," Hazel answered.

Cecilia shook her head. "If it's a good job, you can expect competition to get it. Some of dem people ran away from dat Weaver woman's place, and the law lookin' for them 'cause they agreed to sign contracts and dey left looking for missin' family members. Dats why she shorthanded and always lookin' for help. Did you sign a contract?"

"No."

"I'm stayin' here wit' a man who like my pappy," Bradley said, clinging to Henry's leg. "Tomorrow, we gon' fetch some things from town together."

"Dat ain't your pappy!"

"It is now. I love Brad like he was my blood son. This boy been through enough and want a man to teach him man things."

"Massa Brower sold dis man who took you on like a son, and dat's why he ain't you blood pappy. I love 'em enough to have all my children wit' him, not you or your sister wit' dat yallow skin. I love Henry enough to look at the stars wit' him instead of Massa Brower. I gets to see how God gave me a match and slavery snatched it when I was a young dreamer."

"I don't want to go either. Aunt Cecilia's my best friend. She teaches me things I never knew. I like to learn and she treats me nice." Rosalind stood next to Cecilia.

"You bringin' trouble to dis door and upsettin' everyone who turned into family. Der was no need to talk to or touch dat Weaver woman."

"She don't know which way I went or where I stay."

"You deserve to be more than a washerwoman or whatever that woman had you doin', and dese chillun are blessed with gifts. God is stronger than the clouds of slavery. We don' care about the color of skin 'round here. Nuthin is too difficult for God to mend. Everything was goin' good until dis. You my first love," Henry said.

"And I'm yo last," Cecilia interjected.

"It feels like an evil black cloud hangs over our heads wherever we go," Hazel said with tears.

"I am a man of excellent reputation. If you want to leave like a madwoman and find another White woman who needs domestic workers, just go. You can leave dese kids here wit' us to raise. I reached out my hand to help. No one asked you for nothin'. You not desperate or alone in your situation."

"I stand by my husband's decision. I don't mind if da chil'ren stay while you sort yo' life out right. They'll be well taken care of."

Hazel whispered a silent prayer after thinking over her choice. Then she fell to her knees. "But I's broken. Even my own chillun don' turned against me. All ya faith bigger than mine. I gots to leave Alabama. I been stripped of everything and everyone I love. Stayin' here hurts too bad. I 'preciate everything you and Ceclia done, but I can't bear to be around you no mo'. I was too loyal to John Brower. Cecilia's a good woman. It ain't right to stay here wishin' I was in the bed sleepin' next to you."

25

Wounds of the Past

❧→≫→⋘←❧

"**B**rad and Rosalind, gather your things," Hazel ordered her children. "We're leaving now. This ain't our home; it was just a stop in the road after freedom for us."

Henry sighed, his shoulders slumping in defeat, yet his eyes blazed with frustration. "You gonna leave here and take de children to where? Ain't no easy path out there for a single woman with kids and no money. No one gon' treat yal' better than me and my Cecilia."

"I thought through how we gon' make it. I met someone at a church who told me how to take a train to get to a city called Baltimore in de North."

"You think runnin' away from yo problems in Alabama gon' solve anything? What you gon' do? Have Brad do meat packing, railroad or ship work at the port in Baltimore?"

"Opportunities are better there. De South just tryin' to keep us down."

"Takin' a train don't guarantee a better future. It's a mighty long way."

"But Negro chillun got more places to learn there. They got—"

"Who told you all of dis?"

"I heard about it at a church."

"You ain't got a job, housing or nuthin but you think the world outside of Alabama gon' treat you any better? Travelin' alone not safe. Have you thought of that?"

Hazel clenched her fists. Her decision to leave frustrated her. "I know I can't stay wit' all this heartache. I'm gonna find a way to make it, even if I don't know how yet."

Henry's expression showed both concern and sympathy. He hoped that Hazel and the children could remain in his home with Cecilia, but he knew circumstances made that possibility forbidden. Reality covered on his face.

"You don't trust me enough to work together? You that selfish that Brad and Rosalind gots to suffer because we not together?" he said.

"Dese my kids. I can think whatever I wants to wit' 'em."

"We have a common goal and that's to build up the next generation together. They the ones that gon' help our community do better one day."

"I knew dis was coming. You and Cecilia tryin' to take away my chillun."

"If you can't open yo' mind, walk free, Hazel," Cecilia said. "We not tryin' to do no such thing. Our help has been sincere. There's not been one ounce of false kindness."

"Uncle Henry and Aunt Cecilia helpin' us to get off the bottom. You should be grateful," Bradley reminded.

"Do you want us to fail?" Rosalind added.

"What you're doing to make dem powerless is pure evil. It's sad that you got so much healin' to do that you want to treat these chillun like dey only have a choice to work in a field, work as carriage drivers, housegals or take care of their babies. They come from kings and queens who were wealthy and great workers from de ancient world," Henry added.

"Stop fillin dem chillun's heads wit' dem ridiculous lies!"

"Negroes didn't start in America. Our history started before we had chains. We weren't always property."

"I's poor and they is too. We all came from slaves. I neva seen one queen or king in dis here family of mine," Hazel said sassily.

Henry shook his head. "You're a strong woman, Hazel, but sometimes strength is about lettin' folks help you when you need it, and you should learn more about your people."

"She don't see us as family. All she can think about is not being married to you," Cecilia claimed.

Hazel shook her head, tears streaming down her face. "When Henry was sold, a piece of me died at Rutherford Rocks. I gotta find my own way now for me and for my babies. I can't stay here and keep wishin' for somethin' that ain't never gonna be wit' a married man who has pity on us. I's appreciate you and Cecilia for everything you done, but we gots to go."

"What about that footrace and fishin' trip we supposed to have tomorrow, Uncle Henry? My momma can't give me that. When we were gettin' water down in the spring, we talked and you told me we could start selling produce bags from vegetables we been raising. You said we could get the business off da ground and start delivering to homes wit' your wagon."

The wooden plank floors creaked when Henry grabbed Bradley by the shoulders. He looked him in the eyes. "I love you like you my own boy but your momma said you can't stay," Henry explained.

Tears streamed down Brad's golden-colored face. He hugged Henry as tightly as he could, leaving Henry to wish he could've held Bradley in his arms when he was a baby.

Rosalind had run over to the fresh flowers she had picked. She sobbed as she smelled them, remembering that she'd given a bunch to Aunt Cecilia. She'd given her an identity, a sense of belonging, and a place to call home. Cecilia walked toward her with light steps and a heavy heart.

"You so smart, you little feisty, Missus. When you get to Baltimore, don't forget all the things you learned. Go to school. It is true that there are colleges that might take you on in Baltimore? Fight back by movin' up. When you break a curse, you save a life. Think of chillun who will come after you. Make the best of where you goin' next."

"My momma is trying to strip me and my brother of a better future."

In anger, she turned to Hazel. "I am not here for yo' entertainment. I here to make a difference in the world."

"Don't sass and poke yo' nose in grown folks' business. Ain't no time to fight against each other when gettin' stuck in disobedience will lead to total failure," Cecilia said.

"Tell my momma 'cause her ignorance gon' kill us."

"If your momma refuse to lissen, 'taint nothin' I can do. Pull yoself together and keep respecting your momma 'cause God's in charge and she's next. She got a right to take you wherever she wants you to go," Cecilia reminded.

Cecilia felt afraid and disappointed. She arranged and rearranged items in the parlor, feeling like she was waiting for a large bubble to pop and consume her. Although Cecilia wished the two children she adored could stay, she had no place to challenge Hazel. Cecilia longed for children that she never had.

She felt like an overwhelmed orphan when Rosalind turned to Hazel, her voice trembling with fear and disappointment. "Aunt Cecilia and Uncle Henry love us. I never had a home that made me feel like this. I don't want to leave. Please reconsider."

Hazel kneeled, cupping her daughter's face. "I know you feel like saying goodbye to people you love ain't fair, but sometimes a momma like me gotta make hard choices that a gal like you can't understand. Your aunt and uncle do love us, but I's the one who ain't truly wanted 'cause I'm in da way of their peaceful relationship."

Rosalind sobbed with both fists clenched. "Let me stay here where I'm safe and loved! They said you can go without me and Brad."

Hazel wiped away her daughter's tears with a fingertip, drawing her close against her bosom. "Dat ain't gon' happen. No, Momma, gon' say yes to someone else raisin' her chillun. Da sun be risin', and the birds be singin' soon. We gots to go for a heap of good reasons."

Cecilia sighed, handing Hazel a small package of food and money. "I have no business giving you advice about what ta do, but please take dis'. Good luck to y'all."

Hazel reached out to accept the items. "I's thank you for your hospitality and good spirit."

Brad's shoulders slumped. Rosalind followed in silence, her legs feeling like jelly. She followed her headstrong mother out of the front door of the home that had sheltered them. Though the journey ahead seemed difficult and uncertain, she and her brother had no choice but to follow Hazel.

"If you insist on leavin' let me take y'all in my wagon to as close as we can get to da train," Henry said.

"Dat won't be necessary. We can make it on foot. It'll only make it harder for dese chillun to say goodbye."

"When you first turned me down, I asked God to give you your freedom, and he did. Now I'm askin' God to watch over you and dese chillun. Dis door will always be open if you need to come back to Alabama."

With a final farewell, Hazel faced Henry. "We won't be back, but I's thank you from the bottom of my heart."

Hazel nodded, gathering her strength to head toward the old oak tree that marked the edge of Henry's property. As they walked, the crunch of gravel underfoot was the only sound until they reached the boundary.

ꙩꙩ

After walking until sunrise, a knot formed in Hazel's stomach when she heard the rumble of a covered wagon drawn by oxen.

The wagon stopped, and Hazel's heart pounded in her chest like a rhythmic drum. The driver, a former abolitionist, climbed down and marched toward them.

Hazel tightened her grip on Rosalind and Brad, her mind racing with worry. "What's the trouble, Missus?" Hazel's voice trembled. She wondered if the woman would hurt her or the children. Their journey through the night had been tough; she couldn't afford to add trouble to the already arduous trip.

"Some angry folks lookin' for a woman named Hazel. Is that you?" Her voice was sharp and stern.

"Maybe, Missus. It depend on who wants to know."

"There's no need to call me missus, but there's a story going around that money is missing from the White woman's home named Mrs. Weaver."

Hazel's blood felt icy as it ran through her veins. She feared that Mrs. Weaver would have her and her children hunted down or even killed. "I ain't took nothin'—not a red penny. Missus tried to cheat me while I was workin' for her."

The woman nodded. "I believe you because I had a safe house for escaped slaves going North. Mrs. Weaver has done things like this before. You shouldn't be walking these roads alone with two children. Would you like some help?"

Bradley considered their safety and tugged at his mother's dress.

Hazel tilted her head. "Help how?"

"I'm offering a ride."

Bradley tugged at his mother's dress again to warn Hazel that she should be cautious about believing what the woman said.

Hazel bent down to listen to her son. "How do we know this ain't some trick and this woman won't hurt us? Uncle Henry taught me to be careful about who I trust, especially when a stranger offers help. Missus could be trickin' us and takin' us back to plantation land."

Hazel hesitated, unsure if the woman had ill intent. She wished she had a weighty stick or anything to protect them. She had left Henry's with nothing to defend them. "You right."

Hazel stood and raised her chin. "What's your name, and why would you want to help us?"

The woman's eyes seemed kind and sincere. She smiled. "I'm Sarah Ann."

Hazel looked shocked and confused. "Sarah Ann—Missus Catherine's sister from Rutherford Rocks? Dats the only Sarah Ann I ever met."

"You have a keen memory."

Hazel's body shook. "Your sister hated me because of her husband. I don't want no trouble."

Sarah Ann glanced at Bradley and Rosalind. "I know who all of you are. I didn't come to talk about that. There's only one race—the human race. I've spent a chunk of my life fighting for justice so people like you who were victims of slavery could have better lives."

"I believe her," Rosalind blurted out.

"I don't believe anyone asked for your opinion," Bradley added.

"Well, I'm adding it, anyway."

Hazel knew that taking a chance of getting into the wagon was risky, but so was staying put on an isolated route. She took a deep breath to calm herself, weighing her options.

"I can't say I have a choice but to accept your offer. We three headin' to the train to get to Baltimore."

Sarah Ann had already helped many enslaved individuals, as well as free people of color whom slave catchers had kidnapped and sold into slavery. She later met Negroes who were striving for better lives and migrated to cities such as Baltimore, Maryland, a place that had a history of a large free Negro population. There was still a great division between Whites and Negroes, but she didn't feel it was her place to muddy Hazel's dreams or scare hope away from her bones.

"Let me take you. Dangers lurk around every corner, and you won't have a fighting chance to get to Baltimore if you walk alone. It's not safe out here for you and the children. There's always eyes watching, including a sheriff who's married to Mrs. Weaver. I'm delivering some goods, but I'll make room in this wagon. Helping you and your children is the least I can do."

Hazel wasn't sure if she should trust Sarah Ann, a woman who grew up going to countless slave markets where White people bought and sold *Negroes*. Despite Sarah Ann's background, Hazel took the chance to trust her. "Alright then." She ushered the children into the wagon.

"Watch your step," Sarah Ann advised.

"Thank you—not just for what you're doing for us, but for what you're doing to help all my people."

"You should not be thanking me. I vowed to stop profiting from slavery or have anything to do with it, but my family's past allows me to live comfortably."

"You never treated me bad."

Bradley and Rosalind climbed into Sarah Ann's covered wagon. They didn't realize they were kin and shared the same blood as Sarah Ann. Their young, worn, weary minds were unable to process any more adult matters. The children drifted off to sleep despite their uncertain journey ahead. Hazel and Sarah Ann avoided all talk about Rutherford Rocks during their trip together if they could, until a feeling bubbled up in Hazel too strong to remain silent.

"I never thought a White woman, who once owned slaves, would help them to escape the harsh oppression from the South."

"You deserve a chance to start your lives anew," Sarah Ann said.

Hazel learned that slavery was dead and that a change in the old world they'd all left behind had come by force. Sarah Ann stopped her wagon in front of the train station. Hazel shook Bradley and Rosalind to awaken them. Before they stirred, Hazel wanted to find out something that had been gnawing at her mind.

"Can I ask you something personal?"

"You may."

"Why you ain't never get married?"

Sarah Ann looked at Hazel, never pointing out that she would never see her niece and nephew again. The ardent abolitionist had vowed to fight for equality until she drew her last breath. She had paid the price of never having a husband because she was determined to do God's work to atone for what her forefathers had done, but Sarah Ann suppressed the desire that sparked in her to explain her plight to Hazel. Bradley and Rosalind stirred, allowing Sarah Ann to escape the question.

Brad's eyes widened when he saw his first train in person—a railroad mostly built by enslaved people.

"Look at that!"

Rosalind covered her mouth when she saw a train chug while leaving the station. "How can we afford to ride on that steam locomotive?"

Sarah Ann's eyes met Rosalind's briefly.

Hazel clutched the money she'd saved, and Cecilia had given her. "I hadn't thought of how expensive tickets must be for three people."

She also noticed that she didn't see many Negroes leaving the train cars when they stepped off. She dropped her head feeling defeated, like a life raft had floated out to sea before she could grab it.

"What's wrong?" Rosalind asked.

"I don't think we can afford to get to Baltimore."

Sarah Ann touched Hazel's shoulder, hoping that her resentment for Catherine and feelings of hopelessness would dissipate. "This belongs to you."

Hazel's hand shook as she touched the money.

"Brower's will stated that you and your children were supposed to be freed, and your children were to receive inheritance money if he died. My sister stood in the way of you receiving it. I was looking for you not just because of Mrs. Weaver, but I wanted to give what is rightfully yours. This should be more than enough to get to Baltimore and find your way."

Sarah Ann did not explain that she was sharing money from her own inheritance since Catherine had spent all of Hazel's. She was making up for the many misdeeds that were done at a different time while allowing Hazel to keep her dignity.

The day Hazel left Alabama with her children, for the first time in her life, she felt completely free. She threw her hands toward Heaven as tears of joy sailed down her face. "God done worked a mighty fine miracle."

Epilogue

Unfortunately, moving from the South to the North did not provide the opportunities Hazel had hoped for to escape servitude. She was going through the money that Cecilia and Sarah Ann had given her fast. She found herself in need of money, housing, and stability. After arriving in Baltimore, she thought she would find solace in the vibrant community of freedmen seeking to rebuild their lives. Even after she settled in, Hazel could not establish a tight-knit social and work circle. She had never been the head of a household and was now facing the realities of discrimination in the developing Jim Crow Era.

The best that Hazel could do for herself was find low-paying work as a domestic worker for wealthy families in Baltimore and live on the grounds of one of her employers with her children. Hazel never learned to read or write well. She had not seized the opportunity to master those important skills when she had the chance in Alabama. Limited by age, time, and her inability to exercise her power because the emotional chains of slavery still bound her mind, Hazel believed she could do nothing more than clean, sew, and devote herself to Bradley and Rosalind.

She found hope in her two children, whose lack of opportunity diminished as they rose into excellence. What they had learned from the seeds that Henry and Cecilia planted stuck with them and grew to new heights. Hazel never admitted it, but she knew that Brad's desire to pursue entrepreneurial opportunities came from being in Henry's presence. Taking advantage of the initiatives during the Reconstruction Era that were established by the Freedmen's Bureau, he refused to fall victim to being ripped off or penniless his whole life. He successfully opened his own business—a modest but profitable carpentry shop where he could work for himself. His stable endeavor not only provided for himself, his mother, and his sister, but Bradley also established himself as a respected figure in the community while saving money to invest in his next ventures.

After visiting Henry in Alabama to thank him for his fatherly guidance, Bradley and Henry expanded an enterprise, establishing multiple produce stands and carpentry shops in Alabama, and helping formerly enslaved people to get on their feet by dabbling in entrepreneurship under Henry's guidance and Brad's oversight. Henry only trusted Bradley to handle financial transactions. The collaboration brought them closer.

Hazel dismissed the notion that she had missed out on a good man when she realized how much Henry had poured into her children because he loved her enough to build them up.

Before Hazel could work no more, Bradley moved them back to Alabama to support Henry and Cecilia in their old age, along with his mother. Rosalind was driven by the aspirations instilled in her by Cecilia and her mother. She stayed behind and attended college in Baltimore, becoming one of the few women of her time to earn a degree, accomplishing the great feat. Since Rosalind could attend school, her academic journey laid the foundation for her future contributions to society, allowing her to claim her place as a leader and an asset to her race. She embraced her racial identity since Cecilia explained the One Drop Rule to her, warning her that the world would still see her as a Negro woman. When Rosalind graduated and became a teacher, she felt equipped to embody the dreams of a brighter future that Hazel had always wanted for Massa Brower's two children from the plantation.

About the Author

ANDREA BLACKSTONE is a Virginia-based freelance writer, ghostwriter, associate newspaper editor, and media consultant. She majored in English and minored in Spanish at Morgan State University. While attending Morgan, she received numerous recommendations to pursue a career in writing and was the recipient of the Zora Neale Hurston Scholarship Award.

After a two-year stint in law school, she eventually changed her career path. While recovering from an illness, she earned an M.A. from St. John's College in Annapolis, Maryland—ahead of schedule and with honors. Afterward, Andrea became frustrated with her inability to find an entry-level job in her field and briefly considered returning to law school. However, she realized she was happiest when using her writing and research skills.

Jotting down notes on restaurant napkins and scraps of paper became a habit she couldn't shake. One day, while reflecting on her situation, she emptied the contents of a box and discovered an old photograph of herself with the late Alex Haley, taken during the 1980s when Andrea was a shy high school student. In the photo, Alex Haley was reviewing her writing. She was reminded of how her uncle had complimented her work and offered encouraging words, urging her to continue writing. Finding the keepsake felt like a sign—a nudge to follow the path her heart had always known would bring her fulfillment.

Andrea previously wrote both self-published and traditionally published fiction to gain experience in the industry. *The World We Left Behind* is her first historical fiction novel and her first project after a long hiatus from writing books. The story was inspired by her great-grandmother, Queen Jackson Haley, and is a reimagined tale about slavery and the children of the plantation.